Penguin Books
Bachelors Anonymous

P. G. Wodehouse was born in Guildford in 1881 and
educated at Dulwich College. After working for the Hong
Kong and Shanghai Bank for two years, he left to earn his
living as a journalist and story-writer, writing the 'By the
Way' column in the old *Globe*. He also contributed a series
of school stories to a magazine for boys, the *Captain*, in
one of which Psmith made his first appearance. Going to
America before the First World War, he sold a serial to the
Saturday Evening Post and for the next twenty-five years
almost all his books appeared first in this magazine. He was
part author and writer of the lyrics of eighteen musical
comedies including *Kissing Time*; he married in 1914 and
in 1955 took American citizenship. He wrote over ninety
books and his work has won world-wide acclaim, being
translated into many languages. *The Times* hailed him as
'a comic genuis recognized in his lifetime as a classic and
an old master of farce'.

P. G. Wodehouse said : 'I believe there are two ways of
writing novels. One is mine, making a sort of musical
comedy without music and ignoring real life altogether; the
other is going right deep down into life and not caring a
damn . . .' He was created a Knight of the British Empire
in the New Year's Honours List in 1975. In a B.B.C.
interview he said that he had no ambitions left now that he
had been knighted and there was a waxwork of him in
Madame Tussaud's. He died on St Valentine's Day in 1975
at the age of ninety-three.

P. G. Wodehouse

Bachelors Anonymous

Penguin Books

Penguin Books Ltd,
Harmondsworth, Middlesex, England
Penguin Books, 625 Madison Avenue,
New York, New York 10022, U.S.A.
Penguin Books Australia Ltd,
Ringwood, Victoria, Australia
Penguin Books Canada Ltd, 2801 John Street,
Markham, Ontario, Canada L3R 1B4
Penguin Books (N.Z.) Ltd,
182–190 Wairau Road, Auckland 10, New Zealand

First published by Barrie & Jenkins 1973
Published in Penguin Books 1975
Reprinted 1979

Made and printed in Great Britain by
Hazell Watson & Viney Ltd,
Aylesbury, Bucks
Set in Linotype Times

Chapter One

Mr Ephraim Trout of Trout, Wapshott and Edelstein, one of the many legal firms employed by Ivor Llewellyn, head of the Superba-Llewellyn studio of Llewellyn City, Hollywood, was seeing Mr Llewellyn off at the Los Angeles airport. The two men were friends of long standing. Mr Trout had handled all Mr Llewellyn's five divorces, including his latest from Grayce, widow of Orlando Mulligan the Western star, and this formed a bond. There is nothing like a good divorce for breaking down the barriers between lawyer and client. It gives them something to talk about.

'I shall miss you, I.L.,' Mr Trout was saying. 'The old place won't seem the same without you. But I feel you are wise in transferring your activities to London.'

Mr Llewellyn felt the same. He had not taken this step without giving it consideration. He was a man who, except when marrying, thought things over.

'The English end needs gingering up,' he said. 'A couple of sticks of dynamite under the seat of their pants will do those dreamers all the good in the world.'

'I was not thinking so much,' said Mr Trout, 'of the benefits which will no doubt accrue to the English end as of those which you yourself will derive from your London visit.'

'You get a good steak in London.'

'Nor had I steaks in mind. I feel that now that you are free from the insidious influence of Californian sunshine the urge to marry again will be diminished. It is that perpetual sunshine that causes imprudence.'

At the words 'marry again' Mr Llewellyn had shuddered strongly, like a blancmange in a high wind.

'Don't talk to me about marrying again. I've kicked the habit.'

'You think you have.'

'I'm sure of it. Listen, you know Grayce.'

'I do indeed.'

'And you know what it was like being married to her. She treated me like one of those things they have in Mexico, not tamales, something that sounds like spoon.'

'Peon?'

'That's right. Insisted on us having a joint account. Made me go on a diet. You ever eaten diet bread?'

Mr Trout said he had not. He was a man so thin and meagre that a course of diet bread might well have made him invisible.

'Well, don't. It tastes like blotting-paper. My sufferings were awful. If it hadn't been for an excellent young woman named Miller, now Mrs Montrose Bodkin, who at peril of her life sneaked me in an occasional bit of something I could get my teeth into, I doubt if I'd have survived. And now that Grayce has got a divorce I feel like a convict at San Quentin suddenly let out on parole after serving ten years for busting banks.'

'The relief must be great.'

'Colossal. Well, would such a convict go and bust another bank the moment he got out?'

'Not if he were wise.'

'Well, I'm wise.'

'But you're weak, I.L.'

'Weak? Me? Ask the boys at the studio if I'm weak.'

'Where women are concerned, only where women are concerned.'

'Oh, women.'

'You *will* propose to them. You are what I would call a compulsive proposer. It's your warm, generous nature, of course.'

'That and not knowing what to say to them after the first ten minutes. You can't just sit there.'

'That is why I welcome this opportunity of giving you a word of advice. You may have asked yourself why I, though working in the heart of Hollywood for more than twenty years, have never married.'

It had not occurred to Mr Llewellyn to ask himself this. Had he done so, he would have replied to himself that the solution of the mystery was that his old friend, though highly skilled in the practice of the law, was short on fascination. Mr Trout, in addition to being thin, had that dried-up look which so often comes to middle-aged lawyers. There was nothing dashing about him. He might have appealed to the comfortable mother-ly type of woman, but these are rare in Hollywood.

'The reason,' said Mr Trout, 'is that for many years I have belonged to a little circle whose members have decided that the celibate life is best. We call ourselves Bachelors Anonymous. It was Alcoholics Anonymous that gave the founding fathers the idea. Our methods are frankly borrowed from theirs. When one of us feels the urge to take a woman out to dinner becoming too strong for him, he seeks out the other members of the circle and tells them of his craving, and they reason with him. He pleads that just one dinner cannot do him any harm, but they know what that one dinner can lead to. They point out the inevitable results of that first downward step. Once yield to temptation, they say, and dinner will be followed by further dinners, lunches for two and *tête-à-têtes* in dimly lit boudoirs, until in morning coat and sponge-bag trousers he stands cower-ing beside his bride at the altar rails, racked with regret and remorse when it is too late. And gradually reason returns to its throne. Calm succeeds turmoil, and the madness passes. He leaves the company of his friends his old bachelor self again, resolved from now on to ignore scented letters of invitation, to refuse to talk on the telephone and to duck down a side street if he sees a female form approaching. Are you listening, I.L.?'

'I'm listening,' said Mr Llewellyn. He was definitely im-pressed. Twenty years of membership in Bachelors Anonymous had given Mr Trout a singular persuasiveness.

'There is unfortunately no London chapter of Bachelors Anonymous, or I would give you a letter to them. What you must do on arrival is to engage the services of some steady level-headed person in whom you can have confidence, who will take the place of my own little group when you feel a pro-posal coming on. A good lawyer, used to carrying out with dis-cretion the commissions of clients, can find you one. There is a firm in Bedford Row – Nichols, Erridge and Trubshaw, with whom I have done a good deal of business over the years. I am sure they will be able to supply someone who will be a help to you. It won't be the same, of course, as having the whole of Bachelors Anonymous working for you, but better than nothing. And I do think you will need support. I spoke a moment ago of the Californian sunshine and its disastrous effects, and I was congratulating you on escaping from it, but the sun has been known to shine in England, so one must be prepared. Nichols, Erridge and Trubshaw. Don't forget.'

'I won't,' said Mr Llewellyn.

2

Leaving the airport, Mr Trout returned to Hollywood, where he lunched at the Brown Derby, as was his usual custom, his companions Fred Basset, Johnny Runcible and G. J. Flannery, all chartered members of Bachelors Anonymous. Fred Basset, who was in real estate, had done a profitable deal that morning, as had G. J. Flannery, who was an authors' agent, and there was an atmosphere of jollity at the table. Only Mr Trout sat silent, staring at his corned beef hash in a distrait manner, his thoughts elsewhere. It was behaviour bound to cause comment.

'You're very quiet today, E.T.,' said Fred Basset, and Mr Trout came to himself with a start.

'I'm sorry, F.B.,' he said. 'I'm worried.'

'That's bad. What about?'

'I've just been seeing Llewellyn off to London.'

'Nothing to worry you about that. He'll probably get there all right.'

'But what happens when he does?'

'If I know him, he'll have a big dinner.'

'Alone? With a business acquaintance? Or,' said Mr Trout gravely, 'with some female companion?'

'Egad!' said Johnny Runcible.

'Yes, I see what you mean,' said G. J. Flannery, and a thoughtful silence fell.

These men were men who could face facts and draw conclusions. They knew that if someone has had five wives, it is futile to pretend that he is immune to the attraction of the other sex, and they saw with hideous clarity the perils confronting Ivor Llewellyn. What had been a carefree lunch party became a tense committee meeting. Brows were furrowed, lips tightened and eyes dark with concern. It was as if they were seeing Ivor Llewellyn about to step heedlessly into the Great Grimpen Mire which made Sherlock Holmes and Doctor Watson shudder so much.

'We can't be sure the worst will happen,' said Fred Basset at length. A man who peddles real estate always looks on the bright side. 'It may be all right. We must bear in mind that he has only just finished serving a long sentence as the husband of Grayce Mulligan. Surely a man who has had an experience like that will hesitate to put his head in the noose again.'

'He told me that when the subject of his re-marrying came up,' said Mr Trout, 'and he seemed to mean it.'

'If you ask me,' said G. J. Flannery, always inclined to take the pessimistic view, his nature having been soured by association with authors, 'it's more likely to work in just the opposite direction. After Grayce practically anyone will look good to him, and he will fall an easy prey to the first siren that comes along. Especially if he has had a drink or two. You know what he's like when he has had a couple.'

Brows became more furrowed, lips tighter and eyes darker. There was a tendency to reproach Mr Trout.

'You should have given him a word of warning, E.T.,' said Fred Basset.

'I gave him several words of warning,' said Mr Trout, stung. 'I did more. I told him of some lawyers I know in London who will be able to supply him with someone who can to a certain extent take the place of Bachelors Anonymous.'

Fred Basset shook his head. Though enthusiastic when describing a desirable property to a prospective client, out of business hours he was a realist.

'Can an amateur take the place of Bachelors Anonymous?'

'I doubt it,' said G. J. Flannery.

'Me too,' said Johnny Runcible.

'It needs someone like you, E.T.,' said Fred Basset, 'someone accustomed to marshalling arguments and pleading a case. I suppose you couldn't go over to London?'

'Now that's an idea,' said G. J. Flannery.

It was one that had not occurred to Mr Trout, but, examining it, he saw its merits. A hasty conversation at an airport could scarcely be expected to have a permanent effect on a man of Ivor Llewellyn's marrying tendencies, but if he were to be in London, constantly at Ivor Llewellyn's side, in a position to add telling argument to telling argument, it would be very different. The thought of playing on Ivor Llewellyn as on a stringed instrument had a great appeal for him, and it so happened that business was slack at the moment and the affairs of Trout, Wapshott and Edelstein could safely be left in the hands of his partners. It was not as though they were in the middle of one of those *causes célèbres* where the head of the firm has to be at the wheel every minute.

'You're right, F.B.,' he said. 'Give me time to fix things up at the office, and I'll leave for London.'

'You couldn't leave at once?'

'I'm afraid not.'

'Then let's pray that you may not be too late.'

'Yes, let's,' said Johnny Runcible and G. J. Flannery.

3

Mr Llewellyn's plane was on its way. A complete absence of hijackers enabled it to reach New York, whence another plane took him to London, where at a party given in his honour by the Superba-Llewellyn branch of that city he made the acquaintance of a Miss Vera Dalrymple, who was opening shortly in a comedy entitled *Cousin Angela* by a young author of the name of Joseph Pickering.

She was a handsome brunette, as all his five wives had been, and it was not long before her undeniable good looks caused him temporarily to allow the wise words of Mr Trout to pass from his mind, such as it was. It was not till her play had been running nearly two weeks that he realized the advisability of establishing contact with Nichols, Erridge and Trubshaw of Bedford Row, W.C.1.

Chapter Two

On the stage of the Regal Theatre in London's Shaftesbury Avenue Vera Dalrymple and a man in his fifties were rehearsing a scene from *Cousin Angela*, and anyone following the dialogue would have noted that Miss Dalrymple seemed to be getting all the good lines. And such a criticism would have been justified. The actor who was performing with her now had been known to complain that when you played a scene with Miss Dalrymple you might just as well be painted on the back drop.

In the stalls Joe Pickering was being interviewed by a girl so pretty that the first sight of her had affected his vocal chords. Her matter-of-fact briskness, however, had soon restored his composure, and they were now prattling away together like old friends. Her name, he gathered, was Sally Fitch, and she represented a weekly paper he had never heard of. Women's something, but Women's what he had forgotten.

Nature, when planning Joe Pickering, had had in mind something light-hearted and cheerful, and until the rehearsals of *Cousin Angela* had begun this was what he had been. But a sensitive young man whose first play had fallen into the hands of as exacting a star as Vera Dalrymple seldom retains those qualities for long. Quite early in their association the iron had entered into his soul, and with the opening a few days off he was feeling as he had often felt at the end of a strenuous boxing contest.

Sally, who had been probing into his methods of work, touched on another subject.

'Extraordinary how grim a theatre is in the daytime,' she said.

'Grim things go on in it,' said Joe with feeling.

'I wonder some mystery writer doesn't make it the setting for a thriller. This stall I'm sitting in. The perfect place for finding a corpse underneath. A small corpse, of course. A midget, in fact, and one that had stunted its growth by cigarette smoking in boyhood. His size enabled him to hide in the villain's Homburg hat and he overheard the villain plotting, but unfortunately he sneezed and was discovered and bumped off. I'll make you a present of the idea.'

'Thanks. Why did the heavy put the body under the seat?'

'He had to put it somewhere, and anyway that's up to you. I can't do all the work.'

In addition to being pretty she had, Joe thought, a charming voice. At least it charmed him, but not, apparently, everybody, for at this moment another voice spoke from the stage.

'For heaven's sake will you be quiet at the back there. It's impossible to rehearse with all this talking going on.'

'Oh, sorry,' said Joe. 'Sorry.'

'Who was that?' asked Sally, awed. 'God?'

'Vera Dalrymple.'

'Of course. I ought to have recognized her. I interviewed her once.'

'Please!' from the stage.

'Well, we don't seem to be wanted here,' said Sally. 'Let's go into the foyer. Tell me,' she went on, as the door closed behind them, 'what do you think of that gifted artiste? Off the record. Just between you and me.'

It was a question which Joe was well prepared to answer. He did so with the minimum of hesitation.

'Let's say that I think it possible her mother may love her.'

'But not you?'

'Not me.'

'Temperamental?'

'Very.'

'Bossy?'

'Most.'

'Disposition?'

'Fiendish.'

'But otherwise all right?'

'Not at all. She's a line-grabber.'

'A what?'

'She grabs other people's lines and throws the whole show out of balance. Take that bit they're doing now, it was supposed to be the man who was scoring. It linked up with something in the next act. The story depended on it. But a lot she cares about the story so long as she gets the laughs. I had to re-write the scene a dozen times before she was satisfied that she had grabbed everything that was worth grabbing.'

'I've always heard she was a selfish star.'

'Ha!'

'But couldn't you have told her to go and drown herself in the Serpentine?'

'How could I? She's the boss. You wouldn't expect an Ethiopian slave to tell Cleopatra to go and drown in the Nile.'

'I wouldn't have taken you for an Ethiopian slave.'

'Only because I'm a bit blonder than the average Ethiopian.'

'Is she married?'

'Not that I know of.'

'I'm sorry for her husband, if and when.'

'Yes, one does feel a pang.'

'But we can't help his troubles. On with the interview.'

'Must we? I hate talking about myself.'

'I dare say, but you've got to when you're being interviewed.'

'I can't think why your paper wants an interview with me. I'm nobody much.'

'Well, we aren't much of a paper. And you've probably done something besides writing a play calculated to impress one and all. Have you a sideline? You box, don't you?'

'Who told you that?'

'My editress. She's a great boxing fan. She said you won the amateur championship the other day.'

'*An* amateur championship. Middleweight.'

'She was probably in a ringside seat.'

'Odd, her being interested in boxing. Does she perform herself?'

'I shouldn't wonder. Though I imagine past her best. And now let's have a word about Pickering the author.'

Joe shifted uneasily in his seat. He shrank from giving the

floor to the totally uninteresting character she had mentioned.

'There's not much to say. I write as much as I can in the evenings after I leave the office.'

'So do I. What sort of office?'

'Solicitor's.'

'Rather dull. What made you choose that for a life work?'

'I didn't. I was supposed to be going to the Bar, but there was an upheaval in the family fortunes and I had to take a job.'

This silenced Sally for an unusual moment.

'Tough luck,' she said at length.

'It was something of a blow.'

'But how do you come to be able to attend rehearsals if you're in an office?'

'They let me out for the afternoon.'

'I see. Do you like office work?'

'Not much. It's a living, but I wish I had all day to write in.'

'Same here.'

'How's your writing coming along?'

'Not too badly. But I'm supposed to be interviewing *you*.'

'You're the one I'd like to hear about.'

'Oh, well, if you want the story of my life, you may as well have it. Clergyman's daughter in Worcestershire. Broke away from the reservation. Got various jobs. Spent a long time as secretary-companion to Letitia Carberry. Ever hear of her?'

'Not to my recollection.'

'Very active in connection with the Anti-Tobacco League.'

'Then I'm glad I never met her. I know the Carberry type. Fat and bullying everyone she came across.'

'On the contrary, slender and as sweet as pie. Not very intelligent.'

'I should imagine not, if she fired you.'

'What makes you think she fired me?'

'Well, here you are, aren't you, free from her evil influence.'

'The work got too hard for me and she decided to engage a male secretary. I could have stayed on as companion, but she suddenly took it into her head to go and settle in South America, and I didn't want to leave England. Why South America, you ask? Probably because she had heard that a lot of smoking went on there and she hoped to spread the light. We parted on the best of terms. It was rather like a mother bidding farewell to a daughter, or at least an aunt bidding farewell to a niece, not that I've ever seen an aunt bidding farewell to a niece.'

'Much the same as an uncle bidding farewell to a nephew, I expect.'

'And I came to London and eventually landed my present job.'

'Happy ending?'

'Very. I love the little thing. And now for heaven's sake let's hear from you. I suppose this play means a lot to you – your first.'

'It means everything.'

'Well, good luck.'

'Thanks. Have you ever written a play?'

'Now don't get on to me again,' said Sally. 'Correct this impression that I came here to give you material for my biography.'

When she had gone, far too soon in his opinion, it occurred to Joe that it would be as well to make his peace with Miss Dalrymple. He intercepted her as she was leaving the theatre and asked her to lunch. The invitation was well received, but it appeared that she already had a luncheon engagement, with a Mr Llewellyn, a prominent figure in the motion picture world.

Chapter Three

Enthroned in his box at the artists' entrance of the Regal Theatre, Mac the stage-doorkeeper was conscious of a feeling of depression. This was not because he wanted to smoke and was not allowed to but for a more altruistic reason. Beyond the door to his left the comedy *Cousin Angela* by Joseph Pickering was concluding its brief career, and this saddened Mac.

Not that its failure to entertain affected him personally. As he often said, what took place on the other side of that door made no difference to him. Triumph or disaster, socko or flop, he went on for ever like one of those permanent officials at the Foreign Office. But in the course of their short acquaintance he had become fond of the author of *Cousin Angela* and regretted that he had not enjoyed better luck. When he thought of some of the stinkers whose plays had run a year and more at the Regal since he first took office there, he could not but feel that Fate in allowing only sixteen performances to deserving Joe Pickering's brain child had shown poor judgement.

These thoughts were silent thoughts, for he had no one with whom to share them. His only companion was a middle-aged man who was propped up against the wall with his eyes closed and a dreamy smile on his face. One could not have said that the vine leaves were in this man's hair, for he had practically no hair, but it would have been plain to a far less able diagnostician than the keeper of the stage door that he was under the influence of what is technically known as the sauce. American, Mac put him down as, and he marvelled, as he had often done before, at the ability of the citizens of that great country to hoist so many and still remain perpendicular.

Obviously an exchange of thought – what Shakespeare would have called the marriage of true minds – was not to be expected with one so far below the surface, and Mac's meditations had turned to the prospects of a horse, shortly to run at Catterick Bridge, in whose prowess he had a financial interest, when there entered from the street someone younger and considerably more pleasing to the eye than his predecessor. He was indeed spectacularly good-looking – in the fragile ethereal Percy-Bysshe-Shelley way that goes straight to the hearts of women. His appeal to men was less marked, and Mac regarded him with a jaundiced eye.

He said:

'Mr Pickering here tonight, Mac?'

To which Mac replied:

'He's round in front' – which would not have been a bad description of the visitor propped against the wall, who was noticeably stout. Julius Caesar would have liked him.

The ethereal young man withdrew, and Mac returned to his reverie. But he was soon to resume his social life. The door leading to the stage opened, to admit Joe Pickering.

Things being as they were on the other side of that door, Mac did not venture on his usual smile of welcome. His face was suitably grave as he greeted him.

'Hullo, Mr Pickering.'

'Hullo, Mac. Just came to say goodbye.'

'Sorry to lose you, Mr Pickering. Too bad the show didn't click.'

'Yes, it was a disappointment.'

A snore proceeded from the man on the wall. Joe gave him a speculative glance.

'Blotto?' he said, lowering his voice.

'Sozzled,' said Mac with his Flaubert-like gift for finding the *mot juste*. 'He's waiting for Miss Dalrymple.'

'He'll be an entertaining playmate for her.'

'Ah.'

'Not that he hasn't got the right idea. I am about to go and get into a similar condition myself.'

'Now, Mr Pickering.'

'You don't approve of me drowning my sorrows?'

'I think you're taking this too hard, sir. Everyone has flops.'

'I hoped I'd be an exception.'

'Just got to make the best of it.'

'You preach contentment, do you? Like the butterfly.'

'Sir?'

'The toad beneath the harrow knows exactly where each tooth point goes. The butterfly upon the road preaches contentment to the toad. Kipling. All very well for you to talk. You're a happy rollicking stage-doorkeeper without a care in the world.'

'Yes, sir, but don't think I wouldn't have liked something better, if I could have got it. When I came out of the army, there weren't any cushy jobs going, only stage-doorkeeper, so I became a stage-doorkeeper. But you don't find me beefing about my lot. I'd rather be top man at the Bank of England or run a nice little pub somewhere, but I know when I'm well off.'

His eloquence moved Joe. He nodded understandingly.

'You've made your point, Mac, and I stand rebuked. I abandon the idea of drowning my sorrows. No more self-pity.'

'That's it. Stiff upper lip.'

A thoughtful silence fell. Mac broke it.

'You going out front, Mr Pickering?'

'No, I've seen all I want to of this particular drama. Why?'

'I was thinking that if you were going out front, you might run into Sir Jaklyn Warner, Baronet. He was in here just now, asking for you, and you know what a cadger he is. He wants to make a touch. I could see it in his eye. I should say he'd touched everybody in the West End of London since he started hanging round here. He even stung me for a bit the other day. Made me feel like one of a great big family.'

'One touch of Warner makes the whole world kin. He's certainly not one of our better baronets.'

'You can say that again, Mr Pickering. Jak Warner!' said Mac disgustedly, and the man supporting himself against the wall stirred like some Sleeping Beauty coming to life. 'If you want to know what I think of Jak Warner, he's a twister and a louse.'

The man detached himself from the wall. His eyes were now open and his face was stern. He spoke coldly.

'I heard what you said.'

A sharp 'Coo!' escaped Mac. It was as if he had been addressed by a statue or a corpse after rigor mortis had set in. Joe was equally taken aback. The last thing he had expected from this pie-eyed person was coherent speech.

'And,' the speaker continued, 'I am going to knock your block off. Jack Warner is a dear friend of mine. Well, when I say a dear friend, we haven't spoken to each other for three years, but that makes no difference. Anyone I hear aspersing his name, I knock his block off. It is a name at the mention of which men from one end of Hollywood to the other, including Culver City, bare their heads. 'If,' he added, 'they've got hats on.'

'He didn't mean that Jack Warner,' said Joe, the pacifist.

'You keep out of this.'

Joe persevered.

'You were speaking of hats and Hollywood,' he said.' I suppose not many men wear hats there.'

'Very few.'

'The sun is never too hot. No danger of sunstroke.'

'Practically none.'

'But you get a nice tan.'

'Sure. Who's to stop you?'

Joe was relieved. It seemed to him that by cunningly turning the conversation to the weather conditions in Southern California he had averted an unpleasant brawl. Tact, he was thinking, that was what you needed in an emergency; tact and presence of mind.

'It must be wonderful in Hollywood,' he said. 'All those oranges and movie stars.'

With the best intentions he appeared to have chosen the wrong subject for his eulogy. The face of the inebriated friend of Jack Warner darkened, and his mouth twisted as if he had bitten into a bad oyster. His comment on Joe's words could only have been called curt.

'To hell with movie stars!'

'Quite,' said Joe hastily. 'Quite, quite.'

'The scum of the earth.'

'You're probably right.'

'I'm always right.'

'But the oranges. You like those?'

'To hell with them, too. No time to talk about oranges now. I've got to knock this guy's block off.'

And so saying the pie-eyed man approached the window of Mac's box and started to climb through it.

The situation, Joe saw, was one of delicacy, calling for adroit handling by a third party anxious to make sure that neither of the two contending parties did anything for which he would be sorry later. Mac was liable to get into trouble if he indulged in personal strife with visitors, and his opposite number could not fail to regret it if he went about knocking people's blocks off. With laudable promptitude he attached himself to the latter's garments and pulled. To gather him up and escort him to the street door and push him through it was a simple task. It was, he noticed, raining outside, but no doubt his charge would find a taxi before he got too wet. He returned to Mac with something of the feeling of a Boy Scout who has done his good deed for the day.

'Lord love a duck,' said Mac.

'Lord love a duck indeed.'

'You get all sorts.'

'You certainly do. Who was our guest?'

'Couldn't tell you. He gave his name, but I've forgotten it. Loo something.'

'From Hollywood, I gathered.'

'I don't know where he came from, but I wish he'd stayed there. Much obliged to you, Mr Pickering, for acting so prompt.'

'Don't give it another thought. Well, goodbye, Mac.'

'Goodbye, sir. Better luck next time.'

'If there is a next time.'

'Oh, there will be, Mr Pickering. One of these days the sun will come smiling through.'

'Well, I hope it hurries,' said Joe. 'If you meet it, tell it to get a move on.'

He went out into the street and started to walk to the modest flat which he called his home. The rain had stopped, but there were puddles which had to be avoided, and he had just stepped round one of these when a solid object bumped into him, causing him to stagger.

He clasped it in his arms. Tonight appeared to be his night for clasping his fellow human beings in his arms. A brief while before it had been Mr Loo something from Hollywood; now it was Sally Fitch. Some days had passed since their former meeting, but he had no difficulty in recognizing her.

2

'Good Lord!' he said. 'You!'

'Why, hullo,' said Sally.

'Pickering is the name, if you remember.'

'I hadn't forgotten. Thanks for catching me so adroitly.'

'Don't mention it. What were you doing? Practising rustic dances?'

'Staggering. My heel came off.'

'Oh, was that it?'

'I was walking peacefully along, minding my own business, and suddenly *wham*, no heel on right shoe. Interfered with navigation.'

'I can imagine.'

'There'll be a cab along in a minute. Meanwhile, let's have all your news. Been doing any boxing?'

'Not lately. I did think of plugging Vera Dalrymple in the eye, but I let it go.'

'I hope she hasn't ruined your play. How's it going?'

'It's gone.'

'Oh, no!'

'Came off tonight.'

'Oh, I *am* sorry. You must be feeling frightful.'

'I've been cheerier.'

'You seem cheery enough.'

'Just wearing the mask. I've sworn not to indulge in self-pity. After all, there have been lots of fellows worse off than me.'

'I suppose that's one way of looking at it.'

'Take the boy who stood on the burning deck whence all but he had fled. Can't have been pleasant for him.'

'Not very.'

'But I've never heard that he grumbled. And Napoleon. He suffered from chronic dypepsia. Couldn't digest a thing. Every time he got up from dinner he felt as if a couple of wild cats were fighting for the wild cat welterweight championship inside him. And Waterloo on top of that.'

'And probably all he said was *Oo la la.*'

'I shouldn't wonder.'

'Or *Zut.*'

'Yes, possibly *Zut.*'

'And we could go on kidding like this indefinitely, but that doesn't alter the fact that I'm awfully sorry and think you're taking this awfully well.'

'Thanks. That means a lot to me.'

'I hope everything will get better soon.'

'I have it on excellent authority that the sun will shortly come smiling through. And now,' said Joe, 'I'll get you that cab.'

The cab rolled off, and he resumed his homeward journey. There was a letter lying on the floor as he came into the flat, and picking it up he recognized the handwriting of his friend Jerry Nichols, who worked for his father's legal firm of Nichols, Erridge and Trubshaw of 27 Bedford Row.

'Dear Joe,' wrote Jerry, 'If you can get your Simon Legrees to let you off for half an hour on Tuesday morning, come and see me. I think I may be able to put you on to something good. I specify Tuesday because haste is of the essence and I shall be away all Monday. Don't fail, as this good thing looks quite a good thing. Tuesday, remember, not Monday.'

Promising, Joe felt, very promising. Yet, oddly enough, his thoughts as he dropped off to sleep were not of Jerry Nichols but of Sally Fitch.

Chapter Four

Dotted about London in the less fashionable quarters of the town there loom here and there enormous houses which were built at a time when everybody had ten or eleven children, lots of money and vassals and serfs in comfortable profusion. No longer able to be used as private residences, principally because the serfs and vassals now know a thing or two and prefer to make their living elsewhere, some have become blocks of flats, others hostels for students and the younger wage-earners. Each of the latter has a communal living-room and dining-room and each resident his or her bedroom, and the general effect is of an informal and rather cosy club.

One of these younger wage-earners was Sally Fitch, and on the Sunday following the night on which her shoes had proved so untrustworthy she was in her room, discussing with her friend Mabel Potter the latter's marital problems.

Mabel was the secretary of Edgar Sampson the theatrical manager, but leaving shortly to get married, unless she decided to stay on after the honeymoon, and she wanted Sally's views on which course she ought to pursue. Charlie, it seemed, who made quite enough for two in a stockbroker's office, wished her to retire and concentrate on the home, but she wavered because she liked being a secretary.

'Sammy is awfully nice to work for, and you meet such interesting people in a place like that. There was a newspaper man in the day before yesterday who had delirium tremens right in front of my desk. Do you like your work, Sally?'

'I love it.'

'You must meet a lot of interesting people, too.'

'All the time. Have you ever seen an existentialist poet? Well worth a glance. The one I did offered me absinthe, not to mention a weekend at Bognor Regis. And on Tuesday I'm doing Ivor Llewellyn, the motion picture man. He ought to be good. The trouble with the job is that it's so ships-in-the-nightish.'

'How do you mean?'

'You meet someone you like, chat awhile, and part for ever. You never see them again.'

'Well, you can't expect celebrities to swear eternal friendship.'

'A paper like mine doesn't go in much for celebrities, though I suppose Ivor Llewellyn's one. Never heard of him myself. We get the lesser lights. I was thinking of Joe Pickering.'

'Who's he?'

'You see. The name means nothing to you. He had his first play on at the Regal and it flopped. I was awfully sorry for him. I ran into him again last night, but only for a minute. I suppose that's the last time I shall ever see him, and I've never met anyone I liked so much at first sight. We got on like long-lost brothers.'

'Good-looking?'

'Not a bit. He does a lot of boxing, and that's apt to impair the appearance. But I'll tell you something for your files, young Mabel. Looks aren't everything. A cauliflower ear doesn't matter if it covers a warm heart, which I could see Joe Pickering had. He hated being interviewed, but he remained perfectly courteous throughout, even when I was being most inquisitive about his private affairs.'

'Don't you feel awkward, butting in on perfect strangers and asking them about their religion and do they love their wives and what their favourite breakfast cereal is?'

'You get hardened, like a surgeon.'

'Sammy says interviewers ought to be drowned in a bucket. Oh well,' said Mabel, her interest in that branch of the literary world waning, 'carry on if you enjoy it. What do you think I ought to do? What would you do if you were me? About Charlie?'

'You can't go by what I'd do,' said Sally. 'I'm the meek, yielding type. I'd tell myself I had promised to honour and obey the poor fish, so why not get started. I suppose a lot depends on the man. Is Charlie one of those tough domineering characters who thump the desk and shout "Listen to me. Once and for all . . ."?'

'Oh no, he's not a bit like that. He says "Anything that will make me happy".'

'But he wants you to chuck your job?'

'Yes.'

'Then chuck it, honey, chuck it. A man like that is worth making a sacrifice for.'

'I think I will.'

'Do. It means, of course, that your life will lose a little in the way of entertainment, but what of it? I always say that when you've seen one Gentleman of the Press having delirium tremens, you've seen them all. Your Charlie sounds a pretty good egg. The unselfish type. Just the sort of man I'd like to marry myself.'

'Why don't you get married, Sally? You'd probably have the time of your life.'

'No one has asked me, not recently. I was once engaged, but it didn't jell.'

'You quarrelled? Misunderstanding, and both too proud to explain?' said Mabel, who read stories in women's papers like Sally's, when not working or watching newspaper men have delirium tremens. 'Who was he? A curate?'

'Why a curate?'

'Your father was a vicar. You must have been up to your knees in curates. Or was it the doctor?'

'What makes you think that?'

'There couldn't have been a wide selection in a one-horse place like Much Middlefold. Was it – ?'

'The landlord of the village pub? The odd-job man? The school master? No, it wasn't. It was a baronet, my girl, and a seventh baronet at that. Father used to coach a few assorted young men for Diplomatic Service exams and that sort of thing, and Jaklyn was one of them. So we met.'

'That's an odd name.'

'Family name. Handed down through the ages.'

'Did you break it off?'

26

'No, he did. He said it would be years before we could afford to get married, and it wasn't fair to ask me to wait.'

'Then he hadn't any money?'

'No, the sixth Bart had spent it all, backing losers.'

'Is he in London? Do you ever see him?'

'Who's asking questions now? Yes, he's in London, and I see him occasionally. We sometimes go to the theatre.'

'I suppose you've got over it all right?'

'Oh, completely.'

Mabel rose and stretched herself. She said she must be getting back to her room.

'Letters to write?'

'I don't write letters on my day off. The Sunday papers to read. There's a terrific murder in the *News of the World*.'

Left alone, Sally fell into a reverie. It was not often that she found herself thinking of Jak Warner these days, and now that Mabel's inquisitiveness had brought him back into her mind it was with some surprise that she realized that in stating so confidently that his spell had ceased to operate she had been in error. A good deal of the old affection, she discovered, still lingered. A man may not be an object of admiration to severe male critics like Mac the stage-doorkeeper, but if he combines singular good looks with a smooth tongue and a pathetic wistfulness it is not easy for a warm-hearted girl to erase him entirely, particularly if she still sees him from time to time.

Magic moments of those days at Much Middlefold returned to her. Moonlight walks in the meadows. Kisses in the shadows. Drifting down the river in the old vicarage punt. By the time Mabel returned she had fallen into a mood which in anybody else she would have classified as mushy and getting deeper and deeper into that foolish condition.

Mabel's entry acted as a corrective. She had flung the door open with a violence that made the window rattle and was advancing into the room with wrought-up squeaks. She was waving a paper.

'Look at this, Sally!'

'Look at what?'

'It's about you.'

'What's about me?'

'Read this. Where my thumb is.'

Sally took the paper, and instantaneously the past with its moonlight walks and kisses vanished as if turned off with a switch. She had no need to call on Mabel's thumb for guidance. The moment she scanned the page her own name leaped at her.

'Golly!' she said, and Mabel's comment that she might well say 'Golly' was unquestionably justified.

If, the advertisement stated, Miss Sarah Fitch, formerly of Much Middlefold in the county of Worcestershire, will call at the offices of Nichols, Erridge, Trubshaw and Nichols, 27 Bedford Row, she will learn of something to her advantage; and if a girl was not entitled to say 'Golly' on reading that, it would be difficult to see what would entitle her to say 'Golly'.

Mabel's emotion had reached new heights.

'You know what that means, Sally. Somebody's left you a packet.'

Sally had begun to recover from the first dazed illusion that she had been hit over the head with something hard and heavy.

'They couldn't have.'

'They must have. It always means that when lawyers put in that bit about learning to advantage.'

'But it's impossible.'

'Why?'

'Who could have left me anything?'

Mabel had not read women's papers for nothing.

'Your grandfather,' she said with confidence. 'He disinherited your mother for marrying a clergyman when he had got it all lined up for her to marry the Earl of Something. It's happening all the time.'

'Not this time. My grandfather has always been particularly fond of my father.'

'Oh,' said Mabel, disappointed.

'And what's more he's still alive. I had a letter from him yesterday.'

'Oh,' said Mabel.

'And even if he wasn't, he wouldn't be leaving people money. He hasn't a bean except his pension. If you ask me, it's probably a practical joke. It's the sort of thing some of the girls where I work would think funny.'

'But if it was that, they would have cut the thing out and shown it to you.'

'That's true.'

'Anyway, you'll go and see these Bedford Row people?'

'Oh, I'll *go*. I've enough curiosity for that. I'll go on Tuesday morning. I'm not seeing Mr Llewellyn till the evening.'

'Why not tomorrow?'

'I can't tomorrow. I'll be down at Valley Fields. My old Nanny lives there, and I've orders from home to go and see her every week. I missed last time, so I shall have to go twice this week. But don't worry. Nichols, Erridge, Trubshaw and Nichols will still be there on Tuesday.'

Chapter Five

An early hour on Tuesday found Joe Pickering on his way to see his friend Jerry Nichols.

He walked pensively and in a manner more suggestive of a somnambulist than of a vigorous young man in full control of his limbs. Pedestrians with whom he collided nursed bitter thoughts of him, but had they had the full facts at their disposal, they would have realised that he was more to be pitied than censured, for on waking on Sunday morning he had discovered that on the previous night he had fallen in love at what virtually amounted to first sight, and this naturally disturbed his mind and affected his steering.

His predicament was one he would never have permitted to the hero of any of the stories he wrote in the evening after the day's work at the office was done, for he was, though unsuccessful, an artist. Love at first sight, he felt austerely, was better left to those who catered for the Mabel Potters of this world – Rosie M. Banks, for instance, authoress of *Marvyn Keene, Clubman*, and Leila J. Pinkney (*Scent o' the Blossom* and *Heather o' the Hills*).

And yet it had unquestionably happened, however artistically wrong. He had met Sally Fitch only twice, but love, to quote Rosie M. Banks (*A Kiss at Twilight*, Chapter Three), had cast its silken fetters about him. The symptoms were unmistakable.

There is, of course, nothing to be said against love at first – or even second – sight, but if one is going to indulge in it, it is as well to know the name and address of the object of one's devotion. Sally's address was a sealed book to Joe, and though he remembered the Sally part, what followed after that he had completely forgotten. He had even forgotten the name of the paper for which she worked. And while it would no doubt have been possible for him to buy all the weeklies in London and read through them till he found the interview by Sally Whatever-her-name-was, it was more than likely that with his play such a failure the paper that employed her would not have bothered to print the interview.

It was in sombre mood, accordingly, that he arrived at the offices of Nichols, Erridge and Trubshaw. Fortunately his friend Jerry, an exuberant young man who always had cheerfulness enough for two, now seemed to be in even better spirits than usual. He gave the impression, one not shared by his visitor, that in his opinion everything was for the best in this best of all possible worlds. After preliminary greetings, marked for their warmth, he turned the conversation to the subject of his letter.

'Did anything about it strike you, Joe?'

'Only that it was very good of you to bother about me.'

'Nothing peculiar, I mean?'

'No. Was there anything?'

'It was headed Nichols, Erridge, Trubshaw and Nichols.'

'Well, isn't that the name of the firm?'

'Nichols, Erridge, Trubshaw *and* Nichols.'

Joe saw daylight, and his gloom noticeably diminished. He could rejoice in a friend's good fortune.

'Do you mean they've made you a partner?'

'Just that. About as junior as it's possible to be, but still a partner. Bigger salary, increased self-respect, admiration of my underlings, the lot.'

'Well, that's wonderful. Congratulations.'

'Thanks. And thanks for not saying "Why?". But I'll tell you why. I think my father felt that the firm ought to have someone who talked like a human being instead of in the legal *patois* affected by himself, Erridge and Trubshaw, in order to put nervous clients at their ease.'

'Putting anybody at their ease this morning?'

'Only you and a girl who wrote that she would be turning up. But don't let's talk of my triumphs. Let's get on to this Llewellyn thing.'

'The good thing you mentioned in your letter?'

'That's the one. Splendid opening it looks to me. Of course, it's a gamble. But what isn't?'

'Why is it a gamble?'

'Because it means quitting your job, which would put you in a bit of a hole if Llewellyn decided that you weren't the right man. There you would be without visible means of support, and it isn't easy to get visible means of support these days. I don't mind admitting that if I hadn't had a father who's one of London's most prosperous legal sharks, I'd have been hard put to it to secure my three square meals a day.'

'Could Llewellyn make up his mind in a week?'

'I imagine so. Why a week?'

'Because I'm in the middle of my annual fortnight's vacation, so wouldn't have to tender my resignation immediately.'

'That's good.'

'It solved the immediate problem. And now perhaps you'll tell me what Llewellyn wants and who the hell Llewellyn is.'

Jerry seemed surprised.

'Haven't you heard of Ivor Llewellyn?'

'Never.'

'The big motion picture man.'

'Of course, yes. I've seen the name on the screen at the beginning of films. "A Superba-Llewellyn Production".'

'That's right.'

'But why does he want me, if he does want me? To do what?'

'To act as a sort of resident bodyguard, I gathered.'

'To guard him from what?'

'He didn't say. He became a bit coy when I approached that point. But if you go to 8 Enniston Gardens, where he lives, and say I sent you, I imagine he'll tell you.'

'Perhaps secret enemies are after him.'

'Possibly.'

'A man like that must have dozens.'

'Hundreds.'

'All wearing Homburg hats and raincoats.'

'And armed with Tommy guns. Though, if you ask me, he just wants someone on the spot to say "Yes" to him. Anyway, he'll pay a fat salary, so go and see him.'

'I will. And thanks, Jerry.'

'Not at all. I shall watch your future progress with considerable interest.'

'If it simply means saying "Yes", he couldn't get a better man.'

The inter-office communication buzzed. Jerry leaped to it.

'Yes, father? . . . Right away, father. . . . Expect me in half a jiffy, father. That was father, Joe. He wants to see me about something,' said Jerry, and disappeared at a speed that seemed to suggest that when the head of the firm sent for junior partners, he expected quick service.

Joe remained plunged in thought. He was by nature an optimist, and the slings and arrows of outrageous fortune which up to the present had played such a large part in his life had not completely crushed the hope that, as his friend Mac had said, the sun would one of these days come smiling through. And this Llewellyn opening seemed to him to indicate that this was just what the sun had decided to do.

Mr Llewellyn's reasons for requiring his services had still to be made clear. Possibly he wanted someone to dance before him as David danced before Saul, to entertain him with simple card tricks, or merely to be available to tell unwelcome callers that he was in conference, but, broadly speaking, he was plainly in need of a right-hand man, and in Joseph Pickering he would find that he had made the right selection. He saw himself so endearing himself to Mr Llewellyn, rendering himself so indispensable to Mr Llewellyn, that the latter would have no option but to bestow upon him one of the many lucrative jobs which were at the disposal of a magnate of his eminence. This would enable him, his finances placed on a sound basis, to marry the girl he loved and live happily ever afterwards.

He would first, of course, have to ascertain her name and where she lived, which might involve a certain amount of spadework, but this could be done with the aid of private detectives and bloodhounds.

Not a single flaw could he detect in the picture he had conjured up, and he closed his eyes, the better to enjoy it.

It was at this moment that the door opened noiselessly and Sally came in.

2

As Sally advanced into the room, she was feeling nervous, though she could not have explained why. Nothing to be nervous about, of course. Nichols and the rest of them had asked her to call, she had written to say she would be calling, and here she was. All perfectly straightforward. It was just that there is always something in a lawyer's office which gives the lay visitor the uncomfortable feeling that, though things are all right so far, he may at any moment be accused of soccage in fief or something of that sort and find it difficult to clear himself.

It did not make it easier for Sally that the particular lawyer she was visiting appeared to be asleep, worn out no doubt with toiling over the intricate case of Popjoy versus the Amalgamated Society of Woolworkers. But she was a courageous girl, so she said 'Good morning', and Joe leaped as if the simple words had been a red-hot poker applied to the seat of his trousers.

Springing up and turning, he enabled Sally to see his face, and her relief on discovering an old acquaintance, where she had anticipated an elderly stranger with a cold eye and a dry cough, was great. It did not occur to her to look on Joe's presence there as peculiar. He had told her he worked in a solicitor's office, and this was presumably it.

'Why, hullo,' she said.

Joe was for a moment speechless. For the first time in the past two weeks he found himself thinking kindly of Fate. In the matter of three-act comedies Fate might have let him down with a thud, but it had certainly given of its best now. The miracle of having found this girl, first crack out of the box as it were, stirred him to his depths, and he stared at her dumbly. When he recovered speech, it was of a very inferior quality. He said:

'Well, I'll be . . .'

' "Damned" is, I think, the word you are groping for. I suppose it *is* a coincidence.'

'It's the most amazing thing that has ever happened in the world's history.'

It was not in Joe to be dumb or even incoherent for long. He was a resilient young man, and already he had begun to recover, and was feeling his customary effervescent self again. It amazed him that he could ever have been a prey to depression. For him at this juncture the sun was not merely smiling, it was wearing a broad grin, like a Cheshire cat.

'Won't you . . . sit down, as we say in the theatre?' he said.

'Thank you. Had I better start by showing you my birth certificate?'

'Yes, do. People are always asking me if I have read any good birth certificates lately.'

'It proves that I am the Sarah Fitch –'

'Fitch! Of course. Fitch.'

'– formerly of Much Middlefold in the county of Worcestershire whom you've been advertising for.'

'And what's your address?'

'Where I'm living now, do you mean?'

'Exactly. Obviously you aren't in the county of Worcestershire, so you must be somewhere else – as it might be in the metropolis somewhere.'

'Oh, I see. I'm at one of those hostel places, 18 Laburnam Road, up Notting Hill way. Is it important?'

'Very,' said Joe. 'Very.'

He was relieved to know that there would now be no need for the detectives and bloodhounds whose services he had been planning to engage. Detectives and bloodhounds come high.

'Cigarette?' he said hospitably.

'Thanks,' said Sally, and laughed.

'What's the joke?' Joe asked.

'I was just thinking what Miss Carberry would say if she saw me now.'

'You look all right to me.'

'Yes, but I'm smoking.'

'Ah, yes, I remember you told me about her.'

'She caught me with a cigarette once and lectured me till I felt as if I had confessed to murder, arson, mutiny on the high seas and keeping a dog without a licence. So this is where you work,' said Sally, looking about her. 'Pretty snug.'

Joe coughed.

'I'm afraid I must advance a small correction. I don't work here. My overlords are Shoesmith, Shoesmith, Shoesmith and Shoesmith, who operate a bit farther east. I am just a waif washed up at the doorstep of Nichols, Erridge, Trubshaw and Nichols. They let me come in sometimes to get out of the cold when there's a snowstorm outside. As a matter of fact I looked in to see my friend Jerry Nichols. He was summoned to the presence of the big chief a moment ago, but ought to be back soon, and he, I fancy, is the man you want to see if you have important legal business. Have you important legal business? Not that I wish to pry into your affairs.'

'No, I noticed that. It's important to me all right. If I'm the Sarah Fitch they have been advertising for.'

'Bound to be. Birth certificate and everything.'

'And unquestionably formerly of Much Middlefold in the county of Worcestershire.'

'Ask me, the thing's a walkover. No contest. They will be dust beneath your chariot wheels. You must tell me all about it at lunch.'

'Lunch?'

'I forgot to mention that. You are lunching with me at Barribault's grill room at one o'clock. Unless you elect to put in what Shoesmith, Shoesmith, Shoesmith, Shoesmith, Erridge, Trubshaw and both the Nicholses would call a rebuttal.'

'No rebuttal,' said Sally. 'That'll be fine.' And squashed out her cigarette. She had been planning a roll and butter and a cup of coffee at some wayside tea shoppe, and, though she had never been to Barribault's world-famous restaurant, she knew its reputation.

'If I'm late,' she said, 'wait awhile.'

'Till the sands of the desert grow cold,' said Joe.

Jerry came back into the room. He had a relieved look, as if his interview with his father had turned out unexpectedly well. Mr Nichols senior was a perfectionist who, when his son's conduct called for rebuke, never hesitated to speak his mind.

'Oh, there you are, Jerry,' said Joe. 'How was Pop?'

'Very amiable. He only wanted to give me some instructions about a Miss Fitch in case she blew in.'

'This is Miss Fitch, if you mean the one who was formerly of Much Middlefold in the county of Worcestershire.'

'No, really?'

'Absolutely. Birth certificate and everything.'

'Good morning, Miss Fitch. I'm Mr Nichols.'

'Junior.'

'I'm one of the partners.'

'Junior,' added Joe, 'and if you had come in a day or two earlier, he wouldn't have even been that. A splendid fellow, nevertheless, in whom you can place every confidence. I know of no one I would rather show my birth certificate to. Well, as you will have lots to talk about, I'll leave you. Barribault's grill room at one o'clock, to refresh your memory, Miss Fitch. I'll book a table. Goodbye, Jerry,' said Joe, and was gone.

3

'That was Joe Pickering,' said Jerry.

'I know. I interviewed him for my paper.'

'A shame about his play, wasn't it.'

'Ruined by that Dalrymple woman.'

'Oh, really?'

'She pinched lines and upset balances.'

'Too bad.'

'That's not the way to win to success.'

'No,' said Jerry. 'And now – er – ,' he added, feeling that, delightful though this exchange of views on the drama was, his father would have something to say if he caught him exchanging them, 'Shall we – er – ?'

'Get down to what I suppose you would call the *res*? Yes, we ought to, oughtn't we? Why did you want me to come here?'

'It was with reference to the will of the late Miss Letitia Carberry.'

Sally gasped.

'*Late?*'

'I'm afraid so.'

'Oh, I *am* sorry. I was so fond of her, and she was always so kind to me. What was it?'

'Heart, I believe.'

'Oh, dear.'

'Would you like a glass of water?'

'No, thanks. I'm all right.'

There was a silence. Jerry was wishing that the task of breaking the distressing news had been placed in the hands of Alexander Erridge or B. J. Trubshaw. A tear was stealing down Sally's cheek, and crying women always made him feel as if he were wearing winter woollies during a heat wave. But he reminded himself that business was business and that he was a hard-headed partner in a prominent legal firm, and continued.

'Miss Carberry was a very wealthy woman.'

'I know. I used to have to write all the letters about her investments.'

'You were employed by her?'

'For two years, as a secretary.'

'And your relations were always friendly?'

'I was telling Mr Pickering that she was more like a sort of aunt than an employer.'

'Then that accounts for it.'

'It?'

'You *are* the daughter of the Reverend Herbert Fitch, vicar of Much Middlefold?'

'In the county of Worcestershire? I certainly am.'

'May I see that birth certificate for a moment?'

'Here it is.'

'Seems all in order, and as there must be dozens of people in Much Middlefold who will vouch for you, there doesn't appear to be any need for a lengthy ... what's the word?'

'Quiz?'

'Yes, quiz. Though my father would have a fit if he knew I was conducting my investigation so –'

'Informally?'

'Yes, he's rather a man for taking several hours over things of this sort. So is Erridge for that matter, also Trubshaw. I prefer the simpler method – Who are you? What's your name? Can you prove it? You can? Then right ho, we know where we are.'

'It does you credit.'

'Saves time.'

'You aren't going to ask any questions?'

'None.'

'Well, I am. What did you mean by "it"?'

'I don't quite follow you.'

'I said Miss Carberry was like an aunt to me, and you said "Ah, that accounts for it." '

'I was alluding to the terms of Miss Carberry's will. The bulk of her fortune goes to the Anti-Tobacco League.'

'I can understand that.'

'But you are one of the minor beneficiaries.'

'So I do learn something to my advantage?'

'You do indeed, but there are strings attached to it. Tell me, Miss Fitch, are you a smoker?'

'I don't smoke much.'

'It was Miss Carberry's aim to stop you smoking at all, and she has left you this legacy on condition that you don't do it for two years. By which time, she says in her will, "she will have cured herself completely of the vile habit." I wouldn't knock off smoking myself for all the rice in China,' said Jerry, finally abandoning the conversational methods of Erridge, Trubshaw and his father, 'but you may think differently. Twenty-five thousand pounds is a lot of money.'

The room flickered about Sally. A shelf of legal volumes which Jerry had bought to impress visitors rocked as if in an earthquake, and Jerry himself had apparently been wafted back to the 1920s, for he seemed to have broken into the dance, popular in those days, known as the shimmy.

'Twenty-five thousand pounds!'

'A trifle to Miss Carberry. She probably couldn't think lower than that.'

Sally was still shaken. In a less pretty girl what she was doing would have been described as puffing.

'I wish you wouldn't say these things so suddenly. Couldn't you have led up to it by degrees or blown your horn or something?'

'I'm sorry. I thought you would prefer to get the gist without any of the whereases and hereinbefores you'd have got from Alexander Erridge or B. J. Trubshaw. They would have kept you in agonies of suspense for half an hour. My way, you get the drift immediately.'

'I'm not sure I really do. I can't believe it. Twenty-five thousand pounds!'

'And a very posh apartment at Fountain Court, Park Lane. Which, by the way, you will share with a Miss Daphne Dolby, a young lady from the Eagle Eye detective agency.'

Sally stiffened. The light died out of her eyes.

'Oh, no!' she cried.

'I told you there were strings attached to the legacy.'

'I don't want to share any apartments with any Dolbys.'

'Things being as they are, I'm afraid you've got to. I told you the bulk of Miss Carberry's fortune goes to the Anti-Tobacco League. So, if you break the clause about smoking, does your twenty-five thousand, and the Anti-Tobacco League have got their eyes fixed on it. They want to protect their interests, and how can this be done except by having somebody constantly at your side, spying out all your ways as the fellow said, watching to see that you don't sneak a quiet cigarette when you think nobody's looking? It's in the will. I imagine Erridge or Trubshaw, whichever of them it was who drew it up, pointed out to Miss Carberry that such an arrangement was only fair.'

'I don't call it fair.'

'The Anti-Tobacco League do.'

'A detective!'

'But not the sort of detective you're thinking of. You're picturing a hawkfaced female with piercing eyes and a sniffy disposition, who will make you feel it's only a matter of seconds before she slips the handcuffs on you and hauls you off to the jug. She's not like that at all. She's charming, and you'll like her. In a couple of days you'll be calling her Daffy.'

'All the same . . . You say it's in the will?'

'Plum spang in the will.'

"Then I suppose I've no option.'

Chapter Six

Outside the offices of Nichols, Erridge and Trubshaw, now Nichols, Erridge, Trubshaw *and* Nichols, Sally paused for a moment in thought. In preparation for the interview she had put on her best dress, but though becoming it hardly seemed eye-knocking-out enough for the splendours of Barribault's Hotel, where standards were high. She looked at her watch. The morning was still young, and there would be plenty of time to go to the best place in London and buy something really glamorous. Her host had made a considerable impression on her, and she wanted to be a credit to him. Her identity established, Nichols, Erridge, Trubshaw and Nichols had advanced her a generous sum, so no obstacle stood in the way of her scattering purses of gold. She hailed a taxi.

When she came out of the best place in London with her purchase in her arms, the morning had aged a good deal, but not so much as to preclude a quick visit to Fountain Court. She was naturally curious to see her new home, and she had been given the key. She hailed another taxi.

Number 3A Fountain Court took her breath away. Jerry Nichols had described it as posh, and posh it most certainly was. In addition to her money Miss Carberry had had excellent taste. Everything was just right – the furniture, the curtains, the cushions, the rugs, the books, the pictures. To one accustomed to 18 Laburnam Road the effect was overwhelming, and she dropped into one of the luxurious chairs and tried to realize that all this magnificence was hers.

It was only after some time that a less agreeable thought intruded on her reverie, the recollection that with the magnificence went the constant company of an unknown Miss Daphne Dolby. She wondered with some trepidation what sort of a woman this Daphne Dolby would turn out to be, and was enabled almost immediately to discover at least what she looked like, for Miss Dolby entered through the door presumably leading to the sleeping quarters.

In spite of what Jerry had said, Sally had not been able to rid her mind of the picture of a female detective as something formidable and sinister, and seeing this one she was relieved. The newcomer might reveal herself later as the snake in this Garden of Eden, but she looked all right, very attractive, in fact. She was quite young, with a round pleasant face and brown eyes that had none of the piercing quality which one associates with members of her profession. Hers was quite an ordinary appearance, though a physiognomist would have seen in her mouth and chin evidence of determination and a strong will. They were not the mouth and chin of a weakling.

'Miss Fitch, I take it,' she said, 'and if you are going to say "Miss Dolby, I presume", you will be quite correct. Revisiting the old home?'

'Doing what?'

'Isn't this where you worked for Miss Carberry?'

'Oh, no, she bought it after I left her.'

'And kept it on although she'd gone to South America. What a thing it is to have money. How do you like it?'

'It's wonderful.'

'That's how it strikes me. I think we shall be pretty comfortable here. I hope my company won't spoil it for you. I know I'm a pest and a nuisance, but then those in my line of work so often are. I'll be as unobtrusive as I can.'

Sally, who liked nearly everybody, was now quite fond of her visitor. She replied with warmth.

'You aren't a pest and a nuisance at all. I shall enjoy having you here.'

'I believe you mean that.'

'Of course I do. Are you going to crawl about on the floor picking up small objects and putting them carefully away in an envelope?'

'I will if you want me to. Anything to oblige.'

'And you can tell me all about your cases.'

'They aren't very exciting.'

'No Maharajah's rubies and secret treaties?'

'It's quite a dull job really. Mostly leg-work. If your legs hold out, you're all right. And I don't do any of that now. I own the business.'

'How did you rise to such heights?'

'I had influence. My father was a Superintendent at Scotland Yard. When he had to retire, he founded this agency and worked it up into something big. I got him to take me on as an operative, which is how I come to know all about leg-work. I was promoted to a partnership. Father went off to the Channel Islands to grow tomatoes, and I became the boss. Just a story of local girl with lots of pull making good.'

'I wouldn't have thought the boss would have stooped to such a lowly job as watching over me. Sounds more like an assignment for one of the leg-workers.'

'That was Jerry Nichols's suggestion. He told me you would dislike having a female operative on the back of your neck. He was quite right. My female operatives are nice girls, but they have no conversation, while I, as you may have noticed, have plenty, which will make it fine for you in the long evenings.'

'I'm looking forward to it. Is this sort of arrangement usual?'

'I couldn't tell you. I've never come across it before. But you can see the idea. The Anti-Tobacco League want that twenty-five thousand if they can get it, and they haven't a chance of contesting the will, so they pin their hopes on that smoking clause. Greedy pigs, not to be contented with what they've got, but there it is. Anyway, I wish you good luck.'

'Thank you. I'm glad you're on my side.'

Daphne Dolby became suddenly austere. The words seemed to have given offence.

'I'm not on anybody's side.'

'Oh, sorry.'

'My sympathies are with you,' Miss Dolby proceeded, softening. 'I wish you life, liberty and the pursuit of happiness, and I shall give three hearty cheers if you come through, but I'm like the referee in a football game. He can't take sides. He may want the boys in the pink shorts to clobber the lads in the green with purple stripes, but he doesn't allow that to affect his decisions. Same with me. I take my job religiously.'

'I see what you mean. Integrity.'

'Exactly. I may be rooting for you, but if I catch you smoking, don't think I won't denounce you. Duty first.'

'I understand. Thanks for the warning.'

'Not at all. What's that you've got there?'

'My new dress. I'm lunching at Barribault's.'

'Stepping high already? Quite right. Enjoy yourself while you've got it. I shall have a sandwich and coffee at the office. Unless the fellow I'm engaged to takes me out to lunch. I don't think he will. He never has the price. Too fond of backing losers, like his late father. Can I drop you at Barribault's? It's on my way.'

'No, thanks. I'm going back to my hostel.'

'Then I'll leave you. By the way, don't yield to temptation and have a cigarette while my eye isn't on you. I shall be asking you to breathe on me at unexpected intervals.'

'Breathe on you?'

'Routine precaution, just to make sure.'

'You're certainly thorough.'

'I pride myself on it,' said Miss Dolby.

2

Daphne Dolby's first port of call before going on to her office was number 5 Murphy's Mews, which is situated in the seedier part of Chelsea and inhabited by some of the most dubious characters in London. A few may have hearts of gold, but the best that can be said for most of them is that they are not at the moment actually wanted by the police, though it is always a matter for speculation as to when the police may not feel a yearning for their society. One of these was Daphne's betrothed, Sir Jaklyn Warner. He had been living there for some weeks and would continue to live there as long as the rent-collector was prepared to accept charm of manner and glibness of speech as a substitute for cash.

Arriving at the battered front door of number 5, Daphne did not knock on it. Jaklyn, who always felt uneasy when people knocked on his door, had asked her not to. Placing two fingers of each hand on an upturned tongue, she emitted a shrill whistle, and Jaklyn appeared in his shirt sleeves with a glass in his hand.

'Oh, hullo, Daph,' he said. 'Thank God you've come.'

With those who had known them both it was a constant source of debate as to whether Jaklyn was or was not a more slippery character than his late father. Some said Yes, some said No, but it was agreed that it was a close thing, and the opinion of those who had suffered at their hands that the crookedness of each was such as to enable him to hide at will behind a spiral staircase was universally held. The only difference between the two was that the sixth Baronet had been bluff and hearty and had furthered his ends by slapping people on the back, while the seventh achieved his by looking wistful and pathetic.

He was doing so now.

'Daph,' he said, getting the tremolo into his voice which he found so effective in his dealings with women, 'I'm in a terrible hole.'

'Again?'

Over her glass Daphne fixed those clear eyes of hers on him. She had no illusions about the man she intended to marry. Theirs was not one of the great romances. She had become engaged to him because his bride would be Lady Warner, and he had become engaged to her because she had plenty of money.

She was waiting now for the inevitable moment when she would be given the opportunity of transferring a portion of that money from her possession to his.

'It's not my fault this time,' he said. 'I had this tip on a dead cert and the horse won all right, but there was an objection.'

'How much do you want?'

'Ten pounds.'

'That all?'

'Well, actually twenty.'

'I can manage that.'

'Thank God.'

'Merely remarking that after that disaster at Kempton Park you promised never to bet again.'

'I know, I know. But when you're given an absolutely sure thing.'

'Yes, no doubt you acted from the best motives. But I wish you were like the raven.'

'Raven? How do you mean? What raven?'

'The one who said "Nevermore".'

'Oh, yes, I see. Of course. Ha, ha. Good Lord, it must be fifteen years since I heard anyone mention that poem. My old guv'nor used to make me recite it as a kid when he got a bit bottled.'

'I'll bet you had him rolling in the aisles.'

The financial preliminaries concluded, Jaklyn was at his ease and in the mood for light conversation.

'Well, old girl,' he said. 'What's new?'

'My address for one thing. From now on you will find me at 3A Fountain Court, Park Lane. Make a note of it.'

'You're joking.'

'No. That's where I'll be.'

'Have you been left a fortune?'

'Somebody else has, and I shall be living with her. By the way, you must know her, because I saw you together at the theatre one night.' And, she added silently, I bet she paid for the tickets. 'Look in your little black book. You'll find her among the F's. Sally Fitch.'

'Sally *Fitch*? Good Lord.'

'You do know her?'

'I used to know her quite well. Her father was the vicar of a village in Worcestershire and did some cramming on the side. He coached me when I was trying for the Diplomatic Service. Sally Fitch! Well, for heaven's sake. But who on earth would be leaving her ... did you say a fortune?'

'Figure of speech. But certainly not a windfall to be sneezed at. Twenty-five thousand pounds and this flat in Park Lane. I'm living there with her.'

'Why?'

'Because I've been hired to.'

'I don't understand.'

'You don't have to.'

'I can't see how you get into the act.'

'There are certain conditions attached to the legacy, and I'm there to see that she observes them.'

'What conditions?'

'Never mind. They've nothing to do with you. Well, I must be getting along. Heavy day at the office. All sorts of arrangements to make, now that I shall be away so much.'

She left Jaklyn in pensive mood. He was not a man to whom you could mention that a female of his acquaintance had acquired twenty-five thousand pounds and a flat in Park Lane without stirring his brain to activity. Even while his betrothed had been talking the thought had flashed into his mind that if he hurried round to Laburnam Road and asked Sally to marry him, he would have every chance of being successful. They had once been engaged, and surely some of the old affection must still be lingering. And he could picture his astonishment when, nestling in his arms, she informed him that there would be no need for them to live on bread and cheese and kisses as she was now an heiress.

Thus ran his thoughts, and he would have been out of Murphy's Mews and into a cab at lightning speed, had not there occurred at this juncture a sudden knocking on the front door.

It gave him pause. As he had told Daphne, when people knocked on his door he felt uneasy. Who this was, he could not say. It might be the rent-collector, it might be the tailor to whom he was so deeply in debt or somebody hostile from the racing world. Whoever it was, he shrank from meeting him, and as these fellows had a nasty knack of waiting on the pavement outside in the hope of catching him sneaking out under the erroneous impression that the coast was clear, he reluctantly decided to abandon his journey to Laburnam Road and wait till his visitor had gone away.

Consoling himself with the thought that a letter would be equally as effective as a personal interview, he refilled his glass and sat down to write it.

He made it extremely passionate.

3

Sally, her toilet completed, was looking forward to lunch with mixed feelings. The new dress was all that she had expected of it, but she had a haunting fear that she was not going to be at her best. Excited by anticipation of the visit to Nichols, Erridge, Trubshaw and Nichols, she had slept badly on the previous night, and this had resulted in a tendency to yawn. It would be disastrous, she felt, if she yielded to this weakness at the luncheon table. Joe had struck her as an amiable young man, but even amiable young men resent it if the guest they are entertaining yawns at them all the time.

Hoping for the best, she made her way to the front door, and opening it found Mabel Potter playing truant on the other side, wriggling with eagerness to hear the latest news.

'Sally!' cried Mabel. 'I was afraid I had missed you. Are you off to see those lawyers?'

'I've been.'

'What happened? Did you learn of something to your advantage?'

'I certainly did,' said Sally.

She could not have asked for a more receptive audience. Mabel's favourite reading had always been the novels of the Rosie M. Banks and Leila J. Pinkney whose output so offended the artistic soul of Joe Pickering, and in those this sort of thing happened all the time. She would have considered it most unusual if an impecunious heroine had not been left a substantial legacy by someone.

The figure stunned her a little.

'Twenty-five thousand pounds!'

'And a flat.'

'Where?'

'Fountain Court, Park Lane.'

'Sounds terrific.'

'It is.'

'You've seen it?'

'I've just been there.'

'Come along and show me.'

'There's no time.'

'Of course there's time. I only want to look at it. It won't take five minutes.'

It was soon evident, however, that five minutes was an underestimate. 3A Fountain Court fascinated Mabel. She flitted to and fro with squeaks of approval, while Sally, feeling drowsier than ever, sank into one of the deep armchairs and closed her eyes.

It was a disastrous move. When she opened them again, it was with a scream of dismay.

'Oh, heavens! It's two o'clock!'

Mabel Potter, reclining on a neighbouring settee with the air of one who has never been so comfortable in her life, nodded composedly.

'Yes, you had a nice sleep.'

'Why didn't you wake me?'

'It never occurred to me. I could see you were tired out, and no wonder after all this excitement. A good sleep was what you needed.'

'But I've missed my lunch.'

'Lots of doctors say that's a good thing. Charlie often skips lunch. He says it does wonders for him. Makes him bright in the afternoon.'

'He'll think I stood him up on purpose.'

'He? What he would that be?'

'A man named Pickering. He wrote a play and I interviewed him, and I met him again at the lawyers. He's a friend of one of the partners.'

'And you want to see him and explain?'

'And I don't know where he lives.'

'Well, for heaven's sake it's quite simple. You've only got to ask the partner he's a friend of. Ring him up.'

Sally relaxed. Not for the first time she found Mabel's practical way of looking at things helpful. She supposed secretaries of theatrical managers had to be like that.

'Of course. He's bound to know, isn't he? But I must go to

Barribault's first. He may still be there.'

'Pickering?'

'Yes.'

'When were you supposed to meet him?'

'One o'clock.'

'And it's now two fifteen. If he's still there after waiting an hour and a quarter, which'll be an hour and a half by the time you clock in, he must be something quite out of the ordinary.'

And it was as she spoke that it suddenly dawned on Sally that Joseph Pickering most definitely was.

Chapter Seven

Joe was not still there. There are limits to the staying powers of even the most enamoured, and he had eventually been compelled to recognize that this was just another of the slings and arrows and abandon his vigil.

The emotions of an ardent young man who has asked the girl he loves to lunch and has waited an eternity without the pleasure of her company are necessarily chaotic, and he had them all. On the whole bewilderment predominated. She had seemed so friendly, so eager to better their acquaintance. He found it incredible that she could simply have decided on reflection to have nothing more to do with him. But apparently she had, and all that was left to him was to accept the situation, dismiss her if possible from his mind and concentrate on this Llewellyn who, according to Jerry Nichols, was anxious to secure his services. He was now standing outside the door of 8 Enniston Gardens, the bell of which he had just rung.

The door opened, revealing a tall thin man with gentleman's gentleman stamped all over him. He was carrying a suitcase.

Joe said he had come to see Mr Llewellyn.

'Go right in. He's in there.'

'Perhaps you will lead the way.'

'Not me. I'm through.'

'You're leaving?'

'You're right, I'm leaving. Remarks I can put up with. Tantrums I don't object to. But throwing porridge at a man, that I will not have.'

And so saying the tall thin man passed on his way.

He left Joe a little uncertain as to how to proceed. His late companion's remarks had been brief, even terse, but he had said enough to establish beyond a doubt that behind the door which he had indicated with a jerk of the thumb there lurked something rather unusual in the way of prospective employers. He had an unpleasant feeling of being confronted with a situation to which he was unequal, like a nervous knight of King Arthur's court who, having undertaken to engage in personal combat with a fire-breathing dragon, finds that he has forgotten to bring his magic sword along with him. The years rolled away, and he was once more a boy of eleven, standing outside the study of the headmaster of his preparatory school, the latter having announced his wish to see Pickering there after morning prayers.

Rooted to the spot is a neat way of describing his position, and he might have remained so rooted indefinitely had not the door to which the man who disliked having porridge thrown at him had alluded suddenly flown open, the motive power behind it a large stout middle-aged individual with a bald head and a glare like a searchlight.

'Get out,' said this formidable apparition. 'I don't want any.'

Joe, though far from feeling at his ease, was able to say 'I beg your pardon?'

'Whatever it is you're selling. If it's magazine subscriptions to help you through college, I don't give a damn if you never see the inside of a blasted college. Bosher had no business to let you in. Wait there a moment and I'll ring for him to come and throw you out. Where the devil is Bosher?'

'Gone.'

'Gone?'

'With the wind.'

'You mean he's quit?'

'He said that was his intention. He had a suitcase with him.'

The news did not seem to depress the stout man.

'Well, easy come, easy go,' he said.

'He let me in,' said Joe, 'and didn't even start to announce me, so anxious was he to be off and away. I gathered that there had been a little friction.'

'He burned my breakfast cereal, and I threw it at him.'

'Ah, that would account for his peevishness. Many people dislike having breakfast cereal thrown at them. I for one.'

'And who are you?'

'My name is Joseph Pickering. You, I take it, are Mr Llewellyn. I was sent here by Nichols, Erridge, Trubshaw and Nichols. They said you wanted to see me. Which,' said Joe, 'you are now doing.'

A complete change had come over the stout householder. No longer glaring, he reached for Joe's hand and shook it.

'Oh, that's who you are, is it? Glad to meet you, Pickering.'

'Nice of you to say so.'

'I like the look of you. You give the impression of being just the steady level-headed man I require.'

'That's good.'

'Couldn't be better. Sit down and I'll fill you in.'

It was almost with jauntiness that Joe accepted the invitation. The tremors which had oppressed him at the beginning of this interview had vanished as completely as had the recent Bosher, and he saw now that Mr Llewellyn was simply one of those lovable characters who readily exploded but whose explosions, owing to their hearts being in the right place, are sound and fury signifying nothing. He had met them before, and he knew the type. They huffed and they puffed, but you just sat tight and waited till they blew over. As for throwing porridge at the breakfast table, that was a mere mannerism, easily overlooked by anyone broad-minded. He anticipated a happy association with his future employer.

At this point he noticed that his future employer was looking at him with an odd closeness.

'Hey!' said Mr Llewellyn.

'Yes?' said Joe.

'I've seen you before.'

'Really?'

'Where were you on the night of October the fifteenth?'

Joe winced. It was a night of which he did not care to be reminded, the night on which the comedy *Cousin Angela* had breathed its last.

'I was at the Regal Theatre.'

'In front?'

'Talking to the stage-doorkeeper.'

'I thought so. You're the fellow who gave me the bum's

rush when I wanted to knock the stage-door guy's block off. You attached yourself to the seat of my pants and slung me out.'

It was a severe shock to Joe, and had he not been sitting he would probably have reeled. His opalescent dreams of nestling into the position of Mr Llewellyn's right-hand man, no move made on the other's part without consulting him and a princely salary coming in every Friday, expired with a low gurgle. He was not unintelligent, and he knew that in this world a young man has the choice between two forms of self-expression when dealing with an elder whose patronage he is seeking. He can so ingratiate himself with him as to become his trusted confidant, or he can take him by the seat of the trousers and throw him out of stage doors. He cannot do both.

To his astonishment he saw only benevolence in his companion's gaze. If Mr Llewellyn was not looking at him like a fond father at a favourite son, he told himself that he knew less about fond fathers and the way they scrutinized favourite sons than he had supposed.

'Pickering,' said Mr Llewellyn, 'you little know what a signal service you were doing me when you acted as I have described. Your treatment of the script was just what was needed to make it box office.'

It seemed to Joe, though his grasp on the gist was necessarily insecure, that the thing to do was to smirk in a modest but self-satisfied way, as if, while gratified to think that he had been of service to Mr Llewellyn, he had only done what any man would have done. He did so, and Mr Llewellyn continued, 'Critics would call it a coincidence that you happened to be on the right spot at just the right moment, not that critics matter a damn. They all said that my *Two Hearts in Mozambique* was a bust, and it grossed twenty million. How did you come to be at the stage door that night?'

'It was the last night of my play. I had been saying goodbye to the company.'

'You wrote that play?'

'Yes.'

'I saw it three times. Kind of cute I thought it.'

A gush of affection for this discerning man swept through Joe. The mild liking he had been feeling for him almost from the outset of these exchanges became intensified. Anybody who attributed kind of cuteness to *Cousin Angela* was a kindred soul.

'Oh, did you?' he said, beaming.

'With a little fixing it might make a good picture. I don't say great, I don't even say colossal, I just say good. It flopped, yes, but the practised eye like mine can see possibilities in the worst stage flop. We must talk about it later. Meanwhile I'll tell you why you did me such a signal service.'

'Oh, do,' said Joe.

Mr Llewellyn mused awhile.

'The essential thing for you to get into your nut,' he said, having clarified his thoughts, 'is that I am a man whom women find it impossible to resist.'

Joe said, tactfully, that he was not surprised to hear it. He had, he said, surmised as much the moment they met. Something in Mr Llewellyn's eyes he thought it was.

'There's something dominant about you. Like Napoleon.'

'Was he dominant?'

'Oh, very dominant.'

'That's how it's always been with me. The only exception was a school marm I knew when I was a young man in Wales. She refused to marry me until I had got a thorough grounding, as she called it, in English literature. Shakespeare, you know, and all those.'

'School teachers tend to bring shop into their love lives.'

'Yes, the wise man avoids them. But apart from her my batting average has been pretty darned good. Do you know how many times I have been married?'

'I couldn't tell you.'

'Five.'

'I'd call that good going.'

'Remarkable going. I have this unfortunate tendency to propose to them. There always comes a moment when I can't think of anything to say to keep the conversation from conking out, so I ask them to marry me.'

'Which of course they are eager to do.'

'Naturally.'

'I see your difficulty.'

'The problem is how to stop me proposing.'

'That's what you might call the nub.'

'And that's where you come in.'

'I don't understand.'

'You will. When I left Hollywood this time, my lawyer came to see me off. He had seen me through all my five divorces, and he was worried to think that at any moment he might be called on to see me through a sixth. He told me something I hadn't known before, which was that he belonged to a little group calling themselves Bachelors Anonymous and run on the same lines as Alcoholics Anonymous. If you follow me.'

'Yes, I follow you. When a member of Alcoholics Anonymous feels the impulse to have a drink, he collects the other members and they talk him out of it.'

'Exactly. And when a member of Bachelors Anonymous feels the impulse to propose to a woman, he collects the other members and they talk him out of *that*.'

'Ingenious.'

'Very ingenious. But where I'm concerned there's a catch.'

'I'm sorry to hear that. What is it?'

'I'm in England, and there's no branch of Bachelors Anonymous in England. So what my friend advised me to do was to go to a lawyers' firm he recommended and get them to supply me with a sensible level-headed individual who would take the place of Bachelors Anonymous's fellow members. Do you still follow me?'

'Like a bloodhound. You show signs of being about to ask someone to marry you, and this sensible level-headed individual tells you not to be a silly ass.'

'Precisely. No doubt he would put it even stronger and keep on putting it till he saw that he had convinced me and that the peril was past.'

'He would be able to tell that he had convinced you when he noticed that the dominant look had faded from your eyes.'

'So he would. I might have known that you were the man I

wanted by the promptitude with which you acted that night at the theatre. You heard the stage-doorkeeper say I was waiting for Miss Dalrymple, and with your swift intuition you guessed that it was my intention to take her to supper. You knew how dangerous that would be, so you threw me out. It was raining, and you took it for granted that I would fall into a puddle. I did. I was soaked to the skin. Merely pausing to send Miss Dalrymple a telegram saying I had been called away on business, I went home to bed.'

'You were well out of it.'

'I was, and entirely owing to you. You're a one-man Bachelors Anonymous. You knew Miss Dalrymple, and it appalled you to think that I might be going to marry her.'

'No one marries Miss Dalrymple except over my dead body.'

'A very proper sentiment. Pickering, you're hired, and you will take up your duties immediately. You will move in here, of course. We will talk salary later, but I can tell you that it will be substantial. But for you I should now be an engaged man, and I've only just got rid of Grayce. Grayce,' said Mr Llewellyn, becoming reminiscent, 'was probably my all-time low in the way of wives, though many would say that it was a near thing between her and Bernadine Friganza. When I married her, she was known as the Empress of Stormy Emotion, and believe me the title was well-earned. In a single picture, *Passion in Paris*, she used up three directors, two assistant directors and a script girl, and her stormy emotion spilled over into the home.'

'She sounds rather like Vera Dalrymple.'

'And you saved me. How can I ever thank you, Pickering? What does Shakespeare say about a friend in need?'

'Probably something good.'

'I ought to know. When I was under the spell of that school marm, I absorbed Shakespeare till my eyes bubbled, though not knowing what the hell he was talking about half the time. Odd way of expressing himself he had. Take that bit where ... My God!' said Mr Llewellyn, breaking off.

'Now what?'

'I've just remembered that in that telegram I asked Vera Dalrymple to lunch today at Barribault's grill room.'

A sharp spasm of agony passed through Joe, causing him to feel as if some unseen animal had bitten him in a tender spot. The words 'Barribault's grill room' could not be spoken in his presence without taking their toll.

'But it's all right,' said Mr Llewellyn, unexpectedly brightening. 'This makes a neat end to the whole unfortunate episode. A woman will overlook a man standing her up once, but not two days running. She'll be as mad as a wet hen and will write me off as a wash-out. What Shakespeare would call a consummation devoutly to be wished. Very satisfactory. Most satisfactory.'

His complacency offended Joe. He addressed himself to the task of wiping that silly smile off his face.

'How long have you known Miss Dalrymple?' he inquired.

'A couple of weeks. Why?'

'Because you seem to have got an erroneous grasp of her personality. You appear to think she will accept your abrupt disappearance from her life as just one of those things, perhaps dropping a silent tear but taking no further steps. Have you considered the possibility of her calling on you and setting about you with her umbrella? She may not be my dream girl, but she is a fine upstanding woman, fully capable of beating the tar out of you before you could say "Hullo there, good afternoon, lovely day, is it not." It is a point to which I think you should give some attention.'

If he had expected to freeze Mr Llewellyn's blood and make his eyes like stars start from their spheres, as the motion picture magnate's school marm would have put it, he was disappointed. Mr Llewellyn remained calm, even smug.

'Naturally,' he said, 'I had not overlooked that possibility. But when you come to know me better, Pickering, you will realize that I have all the qualities of a great general. I look ahead, I form my plans. I develop my strategy. See that door?'

Joe saw the door.

'If Miss Dalrymple happens to drop in, I shall nip through it, leaving you to deal with her. And let me say, Pickering, that I place her in your hands with the utmost confidence that you will be able to wipe her off my visiting list. Ah,' said Mr Llewellyn as the door bell rang, 'this may or may not be the broad we have in mind, but a good general never takes chances, so, for the moment, good-bye.'

And he disappeared through the door like a diving duck, while Joe proceeded to follow his instructions with something of the emotions of a young lion-tamer about to enter the lion's cage and nervously conscious that he has only got as far as lesson three of the correspondence course which has been teaching him lion-taming. His relations with Miss Dalrymple had never been cordial, and there was every reason to suppose that he would find her now in an even less amiable mood than usual.

He need have had no tremors. It was not Vera Dalrymple who stood on the mat, but Sally Fitch. Sally was as conscientious in her way as Daphne Dolby was in hers. She had promised her editress to interview Ivor Llewellyn today, and the mere fact that she had been left twenty-five thousand pounds was not going to deter her.

Chapter Eight

In the course of the last round of the amateur middleweight boxing final Joe, hard pressed in a corner by an opponent who created the illusion of being all arms like an octopus, had thrown out a right hand purely at random and with little expectation of accomplishing anything constructive and, connecting with his adversary's chin, it had knocked the latter cold.

This had delighted Joe and his supporters, though – showing once again that one cannot please everybody – it had not brought the sunshine into the life of the opponent. For a long time it had been Joe's high spot, but it was now reduced to second place. His emotions on beholding Sally, though somewhat similar, were much more powerful.

Not unnaturally, as has been shown, he had reached the conclusion that her failure to keep their luncheon appointment had been due to the fact that she had already had all the Joseph Pickering she required, but one look at her as she stood there told him how mistaken such a theory was. Her lips were parted, her eyes shining, her whole aspect that of a girl who has found the pot of gold at the end of the rainbow. If she was not glad to see him, he told himself that he did not know a girl who was glad to see a man when he met one.

'Can you ever forgive me?' she said.

He could answer that.

'Don't give it a thought,' he replied.

'I can explain, but I'm not sure the explanation doesn't make it worse.'

'No need to explain. I know what must have happened. You were on your way to Barribault's when you saw a little golden-haired girl in the process of being run over by a lorry. You rushed to the rescue and saved the child but got knocked over and have only just got away from the hospital. Am I right?'

'Not quite. I fell asleep.'

'You . . . What did you say you did?'

'I was tired after a bad night last night and like an idiot I sat down in a very comfortable chair and when I woke up it was two o'clock. I do hope you didn't wait long.'

'About an hour.'

'Oh, how perfectly awful!'

'Quite all right. An hour soon passes.'

'I feel like bowing my head in the dust.'

'No, really. I was quite happy. But if remorse is gnawing you, you can make amends.'

'How? Tell me how.'

'By dining with me tonight.'

'I'd love to.'

'Same place.'

'I'll be there.'

'About half-past seven?'

'Fine. And it's wonderful of you not to be frothing with fury.'

'Not at all. I quite understand. Got to get your sleep. It knits up the ravelled sleeve of care, as Mr Llewellyn's school marm would say.'

The allusion to the school marm was naturally lost on Sally, but she reacted powerfully to the mention of Mr Llewellyn's name.

'Mr Llewellyn! That reminds me. Now perhaps you will solve the mystery that's turning my hair grey. How on earth do you come to be at Mr Llewellyn's place?'

'Quite simple. I'm working for him.'

'What as?'

'General right-hand man.'

'But that's terrific. Then you've given up the solicitor job you didn't like?'

'As of today.'

'Well, that really is good news.'

'Yes, I'm pretty pleased about it.'

'What sort of a man is he?'

'Very amiable. Why? Have you come to interview him?'

'Yes, and I've heard he's a terror.'

'Nothing of the kind. He's a bit apt to throw porridge at people when the spirit moves him, but apart from that he's all sweetness and light. But here he comes now. You'll be able to judge for yourself.'

A moment before, the door which marked the line of Mr Llewellyn's retreat had opened just enough to allow him to put his ear to the crack and hear the voice of the visitor whose arrival had sent him into hiding. Satisfied that it was not that of Miss Vera Dalrymple, he now threw off all concealment and emerged.

'Oh there you are. Come on in,' said Joe hospitably. 'This is Miss Fitch, who wants to interview you.'

'I made an appointment,' said Sally.

'Sure, I remember. Let's got down to it. Pop off, Pickering.'

Joe was glad to do so. If he was to take up residence at 8 Enniston Gardens, it would be necessary to go back to his flat and pack a suitcase. His typewriter and the rest of his belongings could come on later.

'Don't forget tonight,' he said to Sally.

'I won't.'

Joe went out, his heart singing within him. When he returned, Sally had left and Mr Llewellyn was smoking a cigar with the unmistakable air of a man who has just been speaking at length on the subject of The Motion Picture – Whither?

'Nice girl,' he said.

He had broached a subject on which his young right-hand man felt himself entitled to speak with authority.

'Yes,' said Joe, giving the monosyllable a ringing emphasis which must have made his employer feel he was back with the boys at Llewellyn City. 'You speak sooth, I.L., if I may call you I.L. She is the most wonderful girl in the world. Did you notice her eyes? Terrific. Did you observe her mouth? Sensational. Did you get her voice? Like silver bells tinkling across a meadow in the moonlight. And as sweet and kind and lovable as she is beautiful. I'm giving her dinner tonight.'

'Is that so?' said Mr Llewellyn, starting.

'And I shall instruct her to pay no attention to the prices in the right-hand column, colossal though they are at Barribault's, for this, I.L., is an Occasion. Meanwhile I will be unpacking what I've brought for my simple needs. My bulkier belongings will be coming later. Where's my room? Capital,' said Joe, having been informed on this point. 'Did you happen to catch that little dimple in her left cheek? Earth has not anything to show more fair, as the poet Wordsworth said. You probably remember the passage from your school marm days.'

He left Mr Llewellyn looking as if he were taking a screen test and the director had told him to register uneasiness. He had conceived a warm affection for Joe, and it was impossible for one so imbued with the principles of Bachelors Anonymous as himself not to feel concern at this talk of dimples and silver bells tinkling in the moonlight.

It was precisely talk of this nature which would have made Ephraim Trout purse his lips and his colleagues on Bachelors Anonymous purse theirs. Fervently he wished that Mr Trout were here to advise him what steps to take in order to save Joseph Pickering from the peril that confronted him, and at this moment the telephone rang. He went to it, fortified by the reflection that if this were Vera Dalrymple calling to inquire what the hell, he could always hang up.

'Hello?' he said.

'Hello there, I.L.,' said a well-remembered voice.

The voice of Ephraim Trout.

2

Mr Llewellyn quivered from bald head to shoe sole. Direct answer to prayer frequently affects people in this manner.

'Eph,' he cried. 'Is that you?'

'Who else?' said Mr Trout.

'Where are you?'

'Here in London at the Dorchester. I was called over unexpectedly on business, and of course I got in touch with you right away. I naturally wanted to know how you were making out. Did you go to Nichols, Erridge and Trubshaw as I advised?'

'Sure I did, the first moment I got here,' said Mr Llewellyn, feeling it unnecessary to complicate things by mentioning his *passade* with Miss Vera Dalrymple. 'I saw young Nichols, the junior partner.'

'And he provided a bodyguard?'

'That's just what I want to talk to you about.'

'We must fix up a date.'

'Fix up a date nothing. Do it now.'

'I was going with a friend to that exhibition of first editions at Sotheby's.'

'Damn your friends and blast first editions and curse Sotheby's,' said Mr Llewellyn, who, when moved, always expressed himself forcibly. 'If you aren't here in twenty minutes, I'll take all my business away from you and give it to Jones, Jukes, Jenkinson and Jerningham.'

The threat was one Mr Trout could not ignore. Mr Llewellyn's business was extremely valuable to him, and Jones, aided and abetted by Jukes, Jenkinson and Jerningham, had been trying to get it away from him for years.

'I'll be there, I.L.,' he said, and in less than the specified time he was in a chair at 8 Enniston Gardens, and Mr Llewellyn was saying 'Listen', preparatory to cleansing his stuffed bosom of the perilous stuff that weighs upon the heart, as Shakespeare and the Welsh school marm would have phrased it, though Shakespeare ought to have known better than to put 'stuff' and 'stuffed' in the same sentence like that.

'Listen,' said Llewellyn. 'I have a problem.'

'You aren't engaged to be married?' said Mr Trout in sudden alarm.

'Of course I'm not.'

Mr Trout could have criticized the use of the words 'Of course', but he refrained.

'You relieve my mind,' he said. 'I had a dream about you the other night.'

'Never mind your dreams.'

'I dreamed I saw you coming out of the church with your sixth wife under an arch of crossed movie scripts, held by two rows of directors. But you say you aren't even engaged.'

'It's not myself I'm worried about, it's Pickering.'

'Who's Pickering?'

'The man those lawyers sent me.'

'And you're worried about him? Don't you like him?'

'Yes, very much.'

'But he's no good for the job?'

'He's excellent for the job. But a complication has arisen.'

'Which is?'

'He's gone all haywire over a girl.'

'I don't wonder that that worries you. He sounds the very last man you ought to have around you in your delicate condition. Putting ideas into your head.'

'No, there you are wrong, Eph. No danger of that. I told you I wasn't worried about myself. My anxiety is all for Pickering.'

'Why? Is he your illegitimate son or something?'

'No, he's no relation, but I'm as fond of him as if he were. From our first meeting we have got along together like ham and eggs, and I don't want to see him ruining himself at the very outset of his career. He ought not to be dreaming of marriage at his age. He's much too young.'

'How old is he?'

'About twenty-five.'

'He'd be much too young if he were sixty-five.'

'So I wish you would talk to him.'

'I will.'

'You've had so much experience.'

'More than you could shake a stick at in a month of Sundays. We're used to these hot-headed young Romeos at Bachelors Anonymous.'

'They come to you, do they?'

'No, we generally go to them. Word reaches us that some young pipsqueak is contemplating matrimony, and we look him up. We regard him as an out-patient. And I may say that we are nearly always successful. thought it sometimes happens, of course, that the madness has spread too far. Is the name Otis Bewstridge familiar to you?'

'Never heard it.'

'Heir to the Bewstridge Potato Chips millions. When we tried to dissuade him from marrying his fourth show girl, he blacked the eye of one of our members who was reasoning with him. But this was an exceptional case. Generally reasoning does what we want. Tell me about this Pickering. Is his case a severe one?'

'You bet your bottom affidavit it's a severe one. He raves about her eyes.'

'That's bad.'

'He says her voice is like silver bells tinkling across a meadow in the moonlight.'

'That's worse.'

'He also has much to say about the dimple in her left cheek.'

'I don't like the sound of that at all. You say there is no danger of you imbibing his views, but how are we to be certain? I shall take the earliest opportunity of talking to him like a Dutch uncle. Is this he?' asked Mr Trout as a fresh young voice raised in joyous song made itself heard from beyond the door. Mr Llewellyn said it was, and next moment Joe entered, looking like the jovial innkeeper in Act One of an old-fashioned comic opera.

Seeing Mr Trout, he halted.

'Oh, sorry, I.L.,' he said. 'I didn't know you were in conference.'

'Just chewing the fat,' said Mr Llewellyn. 'This is my old friend Trout.'

In his present mood any old friend of Mr Llewellyn was an old friend of Joe's. Nothing could have been more cordial than his manner.

'How do you do?' he said. 'How do you do, Mr Trout? What a beautiful world it is, is it not?'

Mr Trout gave a short dry cough, as if to indicate that he had seen better in his time, but Joe was not to be discouraged.

'Full of love and joy and laughter,' he proceeded, flashing on the lawyer as sunny a smile as had ever been seen in the S.W.7

postal division of London. 'It makes one want to sing and dance and turn handsprings, doesn't it?'

Another short cough seemed to suggest that Mr Trout was conscious of no urge in this direction.

'I'm off to get my hair trimmed. Can't take a girl to dinner looking like an English sheepdog,' said Joe, and with another smile as dazzling as its predecessor he floated from the room.

A weighty silence followed his departure. Mr Llewellyn broke it.

'See what I mean?'

Mr Trout said he did indeed. His face was very grave.

'Got it right up his nose,' said Mr Llewellyn.

'I have seldom seen a case where the symptoms were more clearly marked,' said Mr Trout. 'He is taking her to dinner.'

'That's what he's doing.'

'And getting his hair trimmed into the bargain.'

'You consider that bad?'

'Don't you?'

'I must say it struck me as sinister.'

'Nothing could be more so. The first thing one notices about these young fellows when they go down with the ailment is that they are always getting their hair trimmed. That and having a shampoo and manicure are the infallible signs that the case is serious. A man who has his hair trimmed and his hands manicured before taking a girl to dinner means business. But it's the dinner that does it, of course.'

'I proposed to Grayce at dinner,' said Mr Llewellyn, wincing at the recollection. 'It's the low lighting.'

'That and the music.'

'And the champagne. Pickering is sure to order champagne.'

'He must be stopped. I must call the boys together for an emergency meeting.'

'But aren't they all in California?'

'That's right, so they are. I was forgetting.'

'You could reason with him by yourself.'

'Hardly ever effective. It's the weight of mass argument that gets results. If only Fred Basset and Johnny Runcible and G. J. Flannery were here.'

'But they aren't, dammit, and he's taking the girl to Barribault's.'

'Why do you say that as if it were significant?'

'Because they have a blasted fiddler there who comes to your
table and plays gooey love songs, the sort of stuff that makes a
girl all sentimental and feeling that she wants to marry the
nearest thing in sight. Let that guy get going around them, and
there isn't a hope that she'll turn Pickering down.'

A look of resolution had come into Mr Trout's face. He was
plainly a man who had reached a decision.

'That settles it,' he said.

'Settles what?'

'There is nothing to do but use Method B.'

'Method B?'

'It is not a course of action I am fond of, and we never use it
except in particularly obstinate cases where verbal argument
has failed and the subject is standing firm on his resolve to get
his hair trimmed and take the girl to dinner. Should that happen, we fall back on Method B. We give him a Mickey Finn.'

It was plain from the quick lighting-up of Mr Llewellyn's
face that Method B had his full approval. He was a man prone
to sudden enthusiasms, and while they lasted he was entirely
under their influence. Mr Trout had convinced him that the
only life that held out any hope of happiness was that of the
bachelor, and Joe's open partiality for Sally had appalled him.
If ever a man needed to be saved from himself, he felt, it was
Joseph Pickering.

'That would fix him,' he said, 'fix him good. When I first came
to America, a man I met in a bar slipped a Mickey Finn into
my drink, and I was out for hours. And when I came to, you
could have paraded all the beautiful girls in New York in front
of me and I wouldn't have given them a glance. I seemed to
have lost the taste.'

The brightness of his face vanished. He spoke despondently.

'But we haven't got a Mickey Finn.'

'I have,' said Mr Trout, producing a white pellet from his
vest pocket. 'I always carry a small supply. So do Fred Basset,
Johnny Runcible and G. J. Flannery. The subjects, especially

when young, so often refuse to listen to reason and become violent. It was only by employing Method B that we were able to dissuade Otis Bewstridge from taking his show girl to dinner. Drastic, you may say, but we of Bachelors Anonymous stop at nothing when duty calls. We regard ours as a holy cause.'

It was some time before Joe returned. His delay had been occasioned, he said, by the fact that in addition to the hair trim he had had a shampoo and a manicure. He took up the conversation where he had left off.

'I was speaking, if you remember, Mr Trout, of what a beautiful world this is. With your permission I would like to go deeper into this matter. What makes it so beautiful is that there are so many delightful people in it. Everywhere I went after I had left you I met a series of the most absolute corkers. Take the fellow who trimmed my hair. Many men are standoffish with strangers, but this chap was affability itself. He never stopped talking. He told me the entire plot of a picture he had seen on his night off, and he held me spellbound. I wonder if it was one of yours, I.L. It was about –'

'Have a drink,' said Mr Llewellyn.

'Not a bad idea.'

'I'll fix it for you,' said Mr Trout.

3

Sally was sitting in the lobby at Barribault's, feeling sick. The Texas millionaires and Indian maharajahs grouped at the little tables around her noticed nothing untoward in her appearance, for her emotions did not show on the outside, but it was as though she had swallowed some nauseous draught and was finding it hard to bear up under the effects of it. She was seeing Joseph Pickering as he really was, and the revelation of his true nature was enough to appal any girl who had allowed herself to become fond of him.

Exactly when she had begun to be uneasy she could not have said, but it was probably when she had looked at her watch and seen that the hands pointed to ten minutes to eight. Arriving punctually at seven-thirty, she had been a little surprised not to find Joe already there, but she had taken a seat without any misgivings, for with traffic conditions what they were a man might well be a minute or two behind time. But twenty minutes behind time was another matter.

Her first thought was that he must have had an accident. It was only much later that some evil imp seemed to whisper in her ear the revolting truth. He was not coming. He had never intended to come. This was his way of repaying her for her failure to keep their luncheon appointment.

It seemed incredible that he could have been so petty, yet what other explanation could there be? If he had had an accident, he would have telephoned. Even if the accident had been a serious one and he had been taken to hospital, a doctor or someone would have telephoned. No, he was deliberately standing her up, as Mr Llewellyn would have said, and it was not long before the sensation of nausea gave way to a boiling fury, and it was as Joseph Pickering Ordinaries, once quoted so high, had experienced a sharp drop and were down in the cellar with no takers, that she heard her name spoken and looking up saw Jaklyn Warner.

Jaklyn, though never fortunate enough to penetrate to the ornate grill room, was a frequent visitor to Barribault's lobby, for it seldom lacked the presence of one or two of his wealthier acquaintances who might be good for a small loan if approached with the right wistfulness. And he had never quite lost the hope that one of these nights some big-hearted reveller, mellowed by Barribault's cocktails, might invite him to come along and have a bite of dinner with him.

Tonight he had not seen anyone who looked like a promising prospect, but he had seen Sally, and he lost no time in joining her. His eagerness to ascertain her reactions to that letter of his was naturally acute.

'Why, hullo, Sally,' he said. 'All alone?'

Sally's voice as she replied was bleak.

'Hullo, Jaklyn. Yes, I'm all alone.'

'I wish I could ask you to have dinner with me, but unfortunately I've come out without my money and they don't know me here, so I can't sign the bill.'

'I don't want any dinner. You can see me home, if you like. Not Laburnam Road. Fountain Court, Park Lane.'

'Yes, somebody told me you have moved.'

'I'm living there with another girl.'

'So whoever it was who told me said. Was it her you were waiting for?'

'No, she's gone to a dinner. Something to do with her old school.'

Jaklyn was relieved. He would have found a meeting with Daphne Dolby embarrassing. It is never agreeable for a man who is engaged to one girl and has just proposed to another to find himself in the company of both of them.

They walked the short distance to Fountain Court in silence. Years of studying other people's moods had made Jaklyn an expert on when to speak and when not to, and he could see that Sally was upset about something and not disposed for conversation. It was only when she had opened the door of number 3A and he had followed her into the living-room that he ventured on the question that was occupying his mind to the exclusion of all other thoughts and said:

'Sally.'

'Yes?'

'Er,' said Jaklyn.

He was not sure he liked the way she was looking at him. It seemed to him a speculative look, as if she were weighing him up, and he was a man who preferred not to be weighed up.

And indeed this was what Sally was doing. She had had no difficulty in interpreting that 'Er'. She was to be given the opportunity of putting the clock back and establishing their relations on what might be called the old Much Middlefold basis.

Had this occurred before Joe Pickering had revealed himself as the impossible character he really was, she would have had no hesitation in crushing Jaklyn's hopes with what Mr Trout would have called a *nolle prosequi*, but now she found herself wavering.

What turned the scale was that he was looking so particularly wistful. It was so obvious that all this while he had been eating his heart out for the one girl in his life and now could endure it no longer. Impossible not to be touched by such fidelity, especially when the man you had mistakenly supposed loved you as you had mistakenly supposed you loved him had turned out not so much to have feet of clay as to be clay all the way up. It was not a subject to let her mind dwell on, but she did feel very definitely that a girl idiotic enough to give a thought to Joseph Pickering ought to be placed under some kind of restraint.

She came to a decision.

'I got your letter, Jaklyn.'

'And?'

'The answer is Yes. I'll marry you if you really want me.'

'*Want* you!' said Jaklyn, with fervour.

He had concentrated all his faculties on making this fervour as convincing as possible, but it now occurred to him that it would be judicious before going further to render quite clear his complete ignorance of the change in Sally's financial condition. There must be no suspicion on her part that he was in any way influenced by the fact of her having joined the ranks of the wealthy.

He proceeded to do so, regretting, for it would have been a neat way of putting it, that the popularity of the song of that title made it impossible for him to say that he could not give her anything but love.

'I'm afraid we shall be very poor, darling, but what of that? What's wrong with being poor if you love each other? It's fun. Everything becomes an adventure. The dreams, the plans, the obstacles that must be surmounted – the rich don't have any of that. They don't know how happy you can be in an attic. With a candle by the bed. When you blow out the candle, you make believe you're in a room in a castle with silk hangings and cupids dancing on the ceiling. Wonderful, wonderful!'

He thought for a moment of going on to the crust of bread for breakfast, but was not sure that that might not be overdoing it. Even as it was, Sally showed herself unsympathetic to his poetic flight.

'We shan't be as hard-up as all that,' she said in her practical way. 'I've got twenty-five thousand pounds.'

'What!'

'And this flat.'

Jaklyn was stunned. He stared at Sally dumbly as she told her story. When she had finished, he conceded that this did make a difference as far as their scale of living was concerned, but maintained that it was essentially a triviality.

'After all,' he said. 'Money, what is it? Love is what matters.'

And on this admirable sentiment he took his leave.

4

Daphne Dolby returned shortly after he had left. She was in excellent spirits, having plainly enjoyed the reunion with the comrades of her girlhood.

'Where were you at school, Sally?' she asked.

'I was privately educated, as they say in the reference books.'

'There were times in my early days,' said Daphne, 'when I wished I had been, but I don't know. It wasn't so bad, looking back, and certainly the hell-hounds I used to regard with loathing seem to have improved with age. I loved them all tonight. I'm giving lunch to some of them tomorrow. Care to come along?'

'I can't, I'm afraid. I'd have loved to, but I've got to go to Valley Fields and spend the day with an old nurse.'

'The Nanny of your childhood?'

'Yes.'

'I'm sorry for you. I know those old Nannies. Mine lives in Edinburgh, thank God. She –'

Daphne broke off. She sniffed. A stern look came into her face.

'Sally! You've been smoking!'

'Not me,' said Sally. 'My betrothed.'

'What! You aren't engaged?'

'I am.'

'You've kept that very dark. Since when?'

'It only happened tonight.'

'Who is he?'

'His name's Warner. Jaklyn Warner.'

The announcement caused a brief pause in the conversation. It is always disconcerting for a girl who is engaged to a man to be told by a friend that she, the friend, is also engaged to him. Daphne was less taken aback than most would have been, for she remembered that she had informed Jaklyn of Sally's legacy, and her knowledge of him told her that this was how, given that information, he might have been expected to act. Her illusions where he was concerned were few.

It was, accordingly, with perfect calm that she said:

'Oh, Jaklyn Warner, eh?'

'Do you know him?'

'I've seen him around.'

There was another pause.

'Of course he didn't know about this money of yours?' said Daphne.

'No.'

'Did you tell him?'

'It came out as we were talking. He was saying how hard up we should be, and I thought it would comfort him to mention it.'

'I'll bet he was astounded.'

'He did seem to be.'

'And overjoyed?'

'Not particularly. I don't think he thinks much about money.'

'No, pure spirit, that boy,' said Daphne.

5

There was a pensive look on Daphne's face as she sat in her bedroom after saying good night to Sally. Lightly though she had seemed to take the latter's revelation, it had shaken her not a little. It is disturbing for a girl who has been regarding her engagement as a stable thing, to be terminated by marriage whenever she feels inclined, to find that there is imminent danger of her betrothed making a sudden dash for liberty. Where everything was placid and leisurely rapid action becomes necessary, and nobody likes being hurried.

She blamed herself for yielding to over-confidence where Jaklyn was concerned. She had assumed too readily that he would feel that a fiancée with a prosperous business and always good for a loan would be something to cling to, and though she had had a marriage licence among her effects for some time, she had always been too busy to use it. She did not often do a foolish thing, but she saw that she had done one when relying on Jaklyn to stay where she had put him.

But she was not the girl to waste time in idle regrets. Long before she had switched off the light and climbed into bed she had found a solution to her problem, and next morning Jaklyn, finishing a late breakfast, was surprised by a familiar whistle at his door. Having ascertained by peeping round the window curtain that she was not a bookmaker or a tailor, he opened the door.

Her car was there, and in it, he saw, was a mysterious stranger.

This was an individual who as far as thews and sinews went could have been the village blacksmith or his twin brother, but in the matter of looks fell short of the standards of the lowest beauty contest. His was a face that could never have launched anything like a thousand ships, and something – possibly an elephant – appeared to have sat on it and squashed it. No one broadminded will allow himself to be prejudiced against a fellow-man because the latter has a squashed face, but this squashed face had in addition a grim and menacing look, such as is so often seen on the faces of actors playing bit parts in gangster films, and – possibly inadvertently – he gave the impression that it would take very little to give him offence. He was carrying in his hand a bunch of roses.

'I've come to take you for a ride, Jaklyn,' said Daphne brightly. 'You don't get nearly enough fresh air.'

Jaklyn, who had been eyeing her fellow-traveller with some alarm, relaxed. He had no objection to going for a spin in her car. A very agreeable way of passing the morning, and she would be morally bound to stand him lunch, possibly at one of those excellent hotels at Brighton where they understood lunch.

'That'll be fine,' he said. 'Who,' he added, lowering his voice, 'is the fellow with the face?'

'Cyril Pemberton, one of my operatives. He's coming with us.'

'Coming *with* us?'

'Yes, he's our witness. I meant to have told you before. We shall be stopping off at the registry office and getting married.'

'*Married!*'

'I've been so tied up at the office that I hadn't time to get around to it before.'

'But –'

'Now don't start arguing, dear,' said Daphne. 'Cyril has been looking forward so much to being a witness. He knows what prestige it will give him with the other operatives being chosen to be witness at the boss's wedding. He specially bought those lovely roses. And he has a very violent temper. I mean I don't know what he will do if you spoil his treat.'

Jaklyn did not spoil his treat.

Chapter Nine

It was Mr Trout's healthy practice to take a brisk walk after lunch when the weather was fine. It tuned up his system and imparted a gentle glow. The day following his visit to Mr Llewellyn being adequately balmy, he set off down Park Lane and had reached the neighbourhood of Fountain Court when he observed approaching him the young man Pickering whose acquaintance he had made on the previous evening.

He greeted him with the utmost warmth, and so kindly and paternal was his manner that Joe, whose morale was at its lowest ebb, threw off perhaps five per cent of the gloom which was wrapping him as if in a garment and replied to his 'Ah, Mr Pickering' with an 'Oh, hullo, Mr Trout' which, though in many respects resembling a voice speaking from the tomb in a story by Edgar Allan Poe, was reasonably cordial.

'A lovely afternoon,' said Mr Trout. He felt no embarrassment at this encounter. Members of Bachelors Anonymous never felt embarrassment when meeting those in whose matrimonial plans they had interfered. To him Joe was just another out-patient who had come to him needing treatment, and this treatment he had given him. He experienced no more remorse at having introduced a Mickey Finn into his beverage than would a doctor who had prescribed for an invalid one of those medicines which nearly lift the top of the head off but effect a cure. 'Glad to see that you are restored to health, Mr Pickering,' he said. 'You had some sort of a fit or seizure yesterday. It alarmed me. It alarmed Mr Llewellyn. It alarmed both of us. And what are you doing in these parts?'

If Mr Trout had been a shade less kindly and paternal, Joe might have kept his private affairs to himself, but he was in the frame of mind when anyone really kind and paternal can extract confidences with the ease of a conjuror taking a rabbit or the flags of all nations out of a top hat. He told Mr Trout that he had been calling on a girl, and Mr Trout said 'Oh?' in a disapproving voice, as if he thought that that was no way for a young man to be employing his time when he might have been reading a good book. This talk of calling on girls, too, made him a little anxious. It seemed to suggest that his treatment of yesterday had not been as effective as he had supposed.

'The young lady of whom you were speaking last night?'

'Yes.'

'I trust you found her well?' said Mr Trout stiffly.

Joe gave a sharp yelp like that of some fiend in torment on whose sore toe another fiend in torment has trodden. The irony of the question had touched an exposed nerve.

'I didn't find her at all,' he said. 'She refused to see me.'

'Indeed? Why was that?'

'You remember I was to have taken her to dinner last night?'

'Ah yes. You had your hair trimmed.'

'And a shampoo and a manicure.'

'And then you had this fit or seizure. I begin to see. She went to the restaurant of your selection, but you did not.'

'Exactly. This must have given her a pretty low opinion of me, and I wanted to see her and explain. I went to the address she had given me, but they told me she had moved to Fountain Court or House or whatever the damned thing is called, so I've just been there.'

'And she would not see you?'

'No. She sent out word to that effect.'

'Then you are well out of it, my boy,' said Mr Trout, and went into his routine with the practised smoothness which years of membership in Bachelors Anonymous had given him. He never had to think and pick his words when holding forth on the drawbacks to marriage. The golden syllables came gushing out as if somebody had pressed a button. It was just the same with Fred Basset, Johnny Runcible, G. J. Flannery and all the other pillars of that benevolent group. As G. J. Flannery had once put it, they seemed to be inspired.

'Yes, Pickering, you are well out of it,' said Mr Trout. 'You have had a most merciful escape. Have you ever considered what marriage means? I do not refer to the ghastly ordeal of the actual service, with its bishops and assistant clergy, its bridesmaids and the influx of all the relations you have been trying to avoid for years, but to what comes after. And when I say that, I am not thinking of the speech you would be compelled to make at the wedding breakfast. That and the service that preceded it are merely temporary agonies, and a strong man can fortify himself with the thought that they will soon be over. But what of the aftermath, when you find that you are linked for life, with someone who comes down to breakfast, puts her hands over your eyes and says "Guess Who"? From what you were saying about the dimple on this girl's left cheek I gather that she is not without physical allure, but can she drive a car? Somebody has got to drive the car and do the shopping while you are playing golf. Somebody has got to be able to fix a flat tyre. Letters, too. What guarantee have you that she will attend to the family correspondence, particularly the Christmas cards? Like so many young men,' said Mr Trout, 'you have allowed yourself to be ensnared by a pretty face, never asking yourself if the person you are hoping to marry is capable of making out your income tax return and can be relied on to shovel snow while you are curled up beside the fire with a novel of suspense. Yes,' said Mr Trout, warming to his subject, 'you are one of the lucky ones. If, as you say, she refuses to see or speak to you, you ought to be dancing sarabands and congratulating yourself on –'

'My God!' said Joe.

What had caused the ejaculation had been the passing cab in which was seated an extremely attractive girl with nice eyes and a dimple in her cheek – reading from right to left, Sally en route to Valley Fields to brighten the life of Miss Jane Priestley, her former Nanny. From London to Valley Fields was a journey of about six miles, and until today she had always made it by train from Victoria, but when a girl has twenty-five thousand pounds in or shortly to come into her bank account she can afford to be extravagant.

This explains the hired vehicle, and the fact that after travelling a short distance it was held up in a traffic jam explains why

Joe, after standing congealed for a second or two, had time to leap into another hired vehicle which happened to be passing and shout into the driver's ear those words familiar to all readers of the right sort of book:

'Follow that car!'

The driver was a stout man with a walrus moustache, not that that matters, who when given instructions liked them to be quite clear, with no margin for error. He said:

'What car?'

'The one over there.'

'Which one?'

'The black one.'

'It's a cab.'

'Well, follow it.'

This delay had given Mr Trout time to join Joe in the cab, which he had been glad to do. Eloquent though he had been, he had still much wisdom to impart, and he was determined that Joe should get the benefit of it. But first there was a question to be put.

'Where are we going?' he asked.

It was the first intimation Joe had received that he had a travelling companion. In his perturbed state of mind he had failed to notice that there was a human form seated beside him. The discovery gave him no pleasure, but he was a young man who in all circumstances was polite to his elders.

'I don't know,' he said.

Mr Trout looked disapproving. He may even have clicked his tongue, but if this was the case the roar of London's traffic made the sound inaudible.

'Is it not a point,' he said, 'on which it would be well to come to a decision before starting on a journey?'

Joe saw that explanations would be necessary. He was not feeling as fond of Mr Trout as he had been some minutes earlier, before the latter had leaped uninvited into the seat at his side, but he supposed he was entitled to be taken into his confidence.

'That girl I was telling you about,' he replied. 'She's in that cab in front there.'

Mr Trout looked more disapproving than ever. He was thankful for the impulse which had made him join Joe.

'And you propose to pursue her and insist on a conference?'

'That's the idea.'

Mr Trout was shocked and hurt. Though not a conceited man, he knew that he was recognized by his colleagues in Bachelors Anonymous as in a class by himself in the matter of marshalling arguments against marriage. Fred Basset had often said so. So had Johnny Runcible and G. J. Flannery. It was galling to him, therefore, to find that his recent eloquence had had so little effect. This incandescent young man was plainly still as incandescent as he had been before a word was spoken.

'You were not impressed by my warning?' he said, not attempting to conceal the coldness in his voice. 'My efforts were wasted?'

'Your what?' said Joe.

'I spoke at some length on the folly of plunging into matrimony.'

'Oh, did you?'

'I did.'

'I'm sorry. I missed it.'

'Oh?'

'I was thinking of something else.'

'Oh?'

'You know how it is when you're thinking of something else.'

'Quite,' said Mr Trout icily.

He was deeply offended. He was not accustomed to mixing with deaf adders. Even Otis Brewstridge, though in the end becoming violent, had *listened*. For an instant he almost decided to withdraw from his mission and allow Joe to rush into ruin in the manner popularized by the Gadarene swine. Serve the misguided young fool right, he felt. Then the never-say-die spirit which animated all members of Bachelor's Anonymous asserted itself. It was as though he could hear Fred Basset, Johnny Runcible and G. J. Flannery urging him to have one more try.

'May I resume my remarks?' he said. 'I touched briefly on the more obvious objections to marriage, and later I will go into them again, but at the moment what I would like to stress is what I may call the family peril inseparable from the wedded state. Most girls have families, and why should the object of your devotion be an exception? I very much doubt that you have bestowed your affection on an orphan with no brothers or uncles. You speak enthusiastically of the dimple in her left cheek, but are you aware that statistics show that eighty-seven point six of girls with dimples also have brothers who are always out of a job and have to be supported? And if not brothers, uncles. In practically every home, if you examine closely, you will find an Uncle George or an Uncle Willie, with a taste for whisky and a distaste for work, whose expenses the young husband is compelled to defray. In the vast majority of cases the man who allows himself to be entrapped into matrimony is not so much settling down with the girl he loves as founding a Haven of Rest for the unemployed.'

He paused for breath, and Joe spoke.

'Now where on earth does she think she's going?' he said, once more making it plain that he had not been following his companion's observations with the attention they deserved.

In the course of the last twenty minutes they had passed through Clapham and Herne Hill and were entering a pleasantly wooded oasis, the Valley Fields to which Sally's former Nanny had retired to spend the evening of her days. She lived with her three cats in a semi-detached house called The Laurels in Burbage Road, and when not entertaining Sally occupied herself by reading the Old Testament, from which she could quote freely, and thinking up ways of annoying her next-door neighbour. The latter's dog Percy had fallen into the habit, as dogs will, of chasing her cats, and she resented this keenly. The result had been one of those regrettable feuds from which even earthly Paradises like Valley Fields are not exempt.

Sally's cab was a fleeter vehicle than the one which chance had allotted to Joe, and despite the efforts of the driver with the walrus moustache she was inside The Laurels with the door closed behind her before Joe had entered the home stretch. Arriving, he leaped out, sped up the little front garden and rang the bell. The door opened, and Miss Priestley appeared.

If Joe had been in a less febrile frame of mind, he might have quailed at the sight of her, for like so many English Nannies, engaged for their skill at enforcing discipline rather than any physical charm, the aspect she presented was formidable to a degree. Very tall, very thin, and very stony about the eyes, she bore a distinct resemblance to Lady Macbeth, with a suggestion of one of those sinister housekeepers who figured so largely in the Gothic type of novel popular in Victorian days.

Joe, though she reminded him of a long-ago Nanny who had frequently spanked him with the back of a hair-brush, faced her without a tremor. He was far too preoccupied to allow himself to be disturbed by old memories.

'Good afternoon,' he said.

Miss Priestley had no comment to make on this.

'Can I come in?'

'Pardon?'

'Would you mind if I came in for a moment?'

'Why?'

'It's very urgent that I see the girl who arrived just now.'

His luck was not in. Sally's former Nanny might have been a friendly soul who would have been delighted to do all that was in her power to help a young man who was plainly in love, but in Miss Jane Priestley he had found the precise opposite of this admirable type. Her leading characteristic was a profound distrust of all men. She suspected their motives and eyed them askance. When they came ringing front-door bells and asking to see girls, she knew what they were after. Her eyes, stony enough to start with, became stonier. She said:

'What do you want with her? No good, I'll be bound. I know your sort. You go about seeking whom you may devour. Preying on innocent girls. Going to tell her you'll cover her with jewels. Repent ye,' said Miss Priestley, becoming biblical, 'for the Kingdom of Heaven is at hand. God shall smite thee, thou whited wall. Abstain from fleshy lusts which war against the soul.'

And so saying she went into the house, slamming the door behind her, and Joe tottered back to the cab.

Mr Trout was standing beside it, eager for details. He had

been too far away to catch any of the dialogue, but he had inter-
preted without difficulty the general run of the scene he had just
witnessed.

'Won't speak to you?' he said.

'No. Get in. We're going home.'

'You go,' said Mr Trout. 'I like the look of this place. I think
I'll stroll around a while and go back by train.'

2

In stating that he liked the looks of Valley Fields Mr Trout
had spoken nothing but the truth. He liked its tree-studded
roads, its neat lawns and above all the flowers that bordered
those lawns. It is estimated that more seeds are planted annu-
ally, more patent fertilizers bought and more greenfly rendered
eligible for the obituary column in Valley Fields than in any
other London suburb, and the floral display there in the sum-
mer months is always remarkable.

But when he gave him to understand that he merely proposed to stroll around taking in the many charms of this
sylvan spot, he deceived Joe Pickering. It was his intention,
when he found himself alone, to proceed to The Laurels and
ask to see Sally. The members of Bachelors Anonymous always
liked to know that a case could be filed away as closed, and he
wished to ascertain whether her avoidance of Joe was due to a
temporary tiff which could be adjusted by a couple of kisses
and a gift on the part of the latter of a box of chocolates or
whether she had cast him off for ever. He was, moreover,
actuated by simple inquisitiveness. As nosey a Parker as ever
walked down Hollywood Boulevard, he wanted to see what the
girl who had made such a deep impression on Joe looked like.

The moment the cab was out of sight, accordingly, he trotted
to the front door and rang the bell.

It had been well said that the hour can always be relied on
to produce the man. It now produced the woman. Miss Priestley appeared, fresh from her triumph over Joe, and stood eyeing him with the cold intentness with which Jack Dempsey used

to eye opponents across the ring. This was her first opportunity of seeing Mr Trout steadily and seeing him whole, but already she had decided that she did not feel drawn to him.

Mr Trout, unaware that suavity was going to get him nowhere, was at his suavest. Smiling a courtly smile which went through Miss Priestley like a dagger, he said:

'Good afternoon, madam.'

To this Miss Priestley made no reply.

'Could I speak to the young lady who arrived here just now?'

He could not have asked a more unfortunate question. For a moment, until he spoke, the châtelaine of The Laurels had supposed him to be another of the pests from one of those consumer research organizations which were always sending representatives to ask her what soap powder she used and what she spent on her weekly budget, but this brazen query revealed him as something far worse – a libertine to wit and, because older, worse than the first one.

'No you couldn't,' she said crisply. 'And you ought to be ashamed of yourself. At your age. Old enough to be her father.'

Mr Trout's courtly smile vanished as if it had been rubbed off by a squeegee.

'You wrong me, madam,' he hastened to say. 'I merely wish to –'

'Well, you aren't going to.'

'But, madam –'

'Get thou behind me, Satan.'

Many men would have felt at this point that the talks had reached a deadlock and that it would be impossible to find a formula agreeable to both parties, but Mr Trout was made of sterner stuff. His years of experience had taught him that all men – and this of course included women – have their price. A pound note, he estimated, would be Miss Priestley's. He felt for his wallet, produced one and pressed it into her hand.

'Perhaps this will induce you to lend a kindlier ear to my request,' he said archly, in fact almost roguishly, smiling another of those courtly smiles which, as we have seen, affected her so unpleasantly.

Miss Priestley looked dumbly at the revolting object. When

a woman of high principles has nursed a girl through the storms and stresses of childhood and the moment the latter is grown up is asked to sell her for gold, her emotions are not easy to describe. Foremost among those of Sally's ex-Nanny was a wild regret that she had come out without her umbrella, for it would have soothed her a little to have been able to strike this smooth philanderer over the head with it. Deprived of this form of therapy, all she could do was to hurl the bribe from her as if it had been a serpent and return to the house.

A pound note has many merits, too numerous to go into here, but it has the defect of not making a good missile. This one fell limply at Mr Trout's feet, and as he stooped to recover it a sudden breeze sprang up and lent it the wings of a dove. It leaped in one direction, frolicked in another. It was as if it had got the holiday spirit and was brushing up its country dances for the next dance around the maypole. It could not have been livelier if it had been told that it was going to be queen of the May.

Nor was Mr Trout any less agile. He was not one of those men who part lightly with anything in the shape of currency. He had once spent half an hour on his hands and knees trying with the aid of a walking-stick to retrieve a dollar bill which had gone to earth under a chest of drawers. The present crisis brought out all the huntsman in him. He wanted that pound note and was determined to get it. Wherever it went, he went, and when eventually it sailed over the fence into the next-door garden it seemed only natural to him to follow it. He would, he knew, be offending against the laws of trespass, but his blood was up and he didn't care.

The breeze had dropped and his quarry was lying inert on the little patch of grass outside the front door, an easy prey. Somewhat out of breath but thrilled by the prospect of the happy ending, he advanced on it with gleaming eyes and outstretched hands, and as he did so an odd sound of someone gargling mouthwash in his rear made him turn. With a sinking heart he saw that he had been joined by a dog.

He stiffened, growing colder and colder from the feet upwards. He had never been at his ease with dogs, and this was a particularly formidable specimen of the species – the sort of dog that hangs about on street corners and barks out of the side of its mouth; a dog, more than probably, known to the police. He viewed it with concern, and the dog viewed him with open suspicion.

Percy was the dog's name, and mention was made earlier of his habit of chasing Miss Priestley's cats. But he was not a specialist who confined himself to this branch of industry. Postmen paled beneath their tan when they saw him, and representatives of consumer research firms were equally affected. His guiding rule in life was. 'If it moves, bite it', and it was unfortunate, therefore, that at this moment Mr Trout should have moved. Abandoning the more prudent policy of standing rigid and hoping that he would be mistaken for a flowering shrub of some kind, he thrust forward a trembling hand, an action against which his best friends would have warned him, and said:

'Good dog. Good boy. Good old fellow.'

Percy's liveliest suspicions were confirmed. He had supposed himself to be up against a unit of organized crime, and how right, he felt, he had been. Panic had robbed Mr Trout's voice of its usual suavity. His 'Good dog' had sounded like a threat to take immediate aggressive steps, as had his 'Good boy', and his 'Good old fellow', and Percy had been left in no doubt that he was in the presence of a far more sinister character than any postman or consumer research man. He ranked Mr Trout even higher as a menace to the public weal than Miss Priestley's three cats, dangerous devils though they were.

He acted promptly, for he shared with Napoleon the belief that attack is the best form of defence. Without waiting for Mr Trout to start throwing the bombs of which his pockets were no doubt full he bit the outstretched hand with all the emphasis at his disposal, and Mr Trout uttered a howl which might well have been that of a dozen cats stepped on simultaneously by a dozen men in hobnailed boots. It had the effect of so startling Percy that he took to his heels and disappeared at some fifty m.p.h., while at the same time a woman came out of the house, plainly eager for explanations.

This was Mrs Amelia Bingham, the widow who owned the other half of the semi-detached house inhabited by Miss Priestley and her cats. Mr Trout, seeing her only dimly through the mist of unshed tears caused by Percy's prompt action, would not have been able to describe her, but she was what is generally termed a comfortable woman. A tendency to plumpness made it unlikely that she would ever become Miss Great Britain, or Miss London and Adjoining Suburbs, or even Miss Valley Fields, but she was beyond a question comfortable. She radiated an atmosphere of cosiness. Mr Trout had once got lost on a walking tour on a cold and rainy night and after hours of wandering had come upon an inn, its lights shining through the mists with their promise of warmth and comfort. His first sight of Amelia Bingham filled him with the same feelings he had had then.

Under normal conditions she smiled easily, but she was not smiling now. Knowing that Percy was at large, and hearing that awful cry, she feared the worst.

'Oh dear. Are you hurt?' she wailed, and ran to where Mr Trout was pirouetting like an Ouled Nail dancer with hand to his mouth.

'Madam,' said Mr Trout, removing the hand for a moment, 'I am.'

'Did Percy bite you?'

'If Percy is the name of that homicidal hound, he did.'

'He probably thought you were the postman.'

'If he cannot tell the difference between me and a letter-carrier,' said Mr Trout, who could be terribly bitter when moved, 'he ought to consult a good oculist.'

It was at this point that Amelia Bingham suggested that he should come into the house and have his wounds dressed, and he followed her there. He was still in the grip of the righteous wrath which animates men who have been bitten by dogs to whom they have not done a thing except address them as good boys and good old fellows, but gradually resentment gave way to kindlier feelings. It was impossible not to be soothed by contact with this woman. Very soon conversation was proceeding in the most amicable manner. Amelia Bingham said that Percy was a naughty dog, and Mr Trout said he had already formed that opinion.

'You're American, aren't you?' said Amelia Bingham. 'I thought so. It was your saying "letter-carrier" instead of post-man. Tell me if this hurts,' she said, referring to the iodine which she was applying to his hand.

Mr Trout, his good humour completely restored, assured her that it did not. He also complimented her on the skill with which she was applying the bandage, and she said she had had a lot of practice.

'Bandaging letter-carriers?'

'Not very often, because Percy usually goes for their trousers. I meant at the hospital. I'm a hospital nurse.'

'Ah, that would account for it.'

'This is my day off. We get one a week at St Swithin's. Whereabouts in America do you come from?'

'California,' said Mr Trout with the reverence that always came into his voice when he spoke that name. 'My home is in Hollywood.'

'Oh, are you in the movies?'

'No, I am a lawyer.'

Amelia Bingham uttered a pleased cry.

'Then you can tell me if the woman next door has any right to throw her snails into my garden.'

'None whatever. Legally, snails are wild animals.'

'What ought I to do?'

'Throw them back.'

Amelia Bingham said he had taken a great weight off her mind, and Mr Trout said he was happy to have been able to be of service to her. Their relations were becoming more cordial every moment.

'Is it nice there?' Amelia Bingham asked.

'Where?'

'In California.'

'Very nice. California is generally described as the jewel state of the Union. Bathed in eternal sunshine, cooled by gentle breezes, it affords the ideal dwelling place for the stalwart men and fair women who inhabit it. Its noble movie houses, its spreading orange-groves –'

'How about the earthquakes?'

Mr Trout, who had been waving his hands emotionally, stopped with them in mid-air as abruptly as if he had heard a director say 'Cut'. He stared like one who is having a difficulty in believing his ears.

'I beg your pardon?'

'Didn't you have a bad one some time ago?'

'You are thinking of the San Francisco fire of 1906.'

'Oh, it was a fire, was it?'

'A fire,' said Mr Trout firmly. 'Earthquakes are absolutely unknown in California.'

'One always gets these things wrong. There,' said Amelia Bingham. 'That ought to hold if you don't wave it too much. And now you must let me give you a cup of tea. You would like a cup of tea, wouldn't you?'

'It would be extremely refreshing,' said Mr Trout.

It was over the meal that he first realized that strange things were happening to him this afternoon, strange emotions stirring within him. His whole outlook seemed to have changed. As he watched his hostess sip her tea and tucked into the superlative scones which, he learned, were of her own baking, he became more and more convinced that for the last twenty years he had been proceeding on entirely wrong lines. In supposing that the bachelor's was the ideal life he had been guilty of a gross error. More and more clearly as the scones disappeared into his interior he saw that what the sensible man wanted was a wife and a home with scones like these always at his disposal. He had, in a word, like Romeo, Joe Pickering and other notabilities, fallen in love at first sight, and if any thought of Fred Basset, Johnny Runcible and G. J. Flannery came into his mind, he dismissed it without a qualm.

It seems to be a law of Nature that when a confirmed bachelor falls in love, he does it with a wholeheartedness beyond the scope of the ordinary man who has been scattering his affections hither and thither since he was so high, As a child of eight Mr Trout had once kissed a girl of six under the mistletoe at a

Christmas party, but there his sex life had come to an abrupt halt, with the result that for forty years passion had been banking up inside him like water in a dam. Sooner or later the dam was bound to burst, and his meeting with Amelia Bingham had brought this about. Quite suddenly he found himself abandoning all the principles of a lifetime. No longer the silver-tongued denouncer of love at whom the personnel of Bachelors Anonymous pointed with pride, he yearned for Amelia Bingham as harts are said to yearn for waterbrooks. If somebody had happened to come along at this moment bearing a sprig of mistletoe, he would have kissed her under it without hesitation.

'Delicious,' he said, swallowing the last scone. 'You really baked these yourself?'

'And made the strawberry jam.'

'Amazing. You must allow me to make some return for your hospitality. Could I persuade you to dine with me tonight?'

'I should love it.'

'I am staying at the Dorchester. Shall we dine there? At about seven-thirty?'

'Splendid.'

'Don't bring Percy with you,' said Mr Trout. 'Ha ha,' he added, to show that this was whimsical humour.

'Ha, ha,' said Amelia Bingham.

'Ho, ho,' said Mr Trout.

He made a mental note to get his hair trimmed and to have a manicure and a shampoo.

Chapter Ten

The late afternoon of the day on which love had come to Mr Trout found Ivor Llewellyn in the best of spirits. His intention of putting a stick of dynamite beneath the pants of his London employees had been amply fulfilled; the cook he had engaged was proving excellent; a transatlantic telephone call to the studio had assured him that all was going well there in his absence; and he had not heard a word from Vera Dalrymple. Providence, he felt, was going out of its way to make things pleasant for a good man.

It was the last item on this list that set the seal on his well-being. As the days went by, he had become more and more alive to the perils inseparable from association with Miss Dalrymple. Twice since their first meeting he had come within a hair's breadth of proposing marriage to her, and only the merest chance had averted disaster. Once a table-hopping friend of hers had interrupted him as the fatal words were trembling on his lips; on the other occasion he had been saved by a sudden attack of hiccups, giving him time to reflect while the waiter was patting him on the back.

But he knew that luck like this could not last if he continued to see her, and the fact that there had been no communication on her part put new heart into him. At their last dinner together he had been appalled to notice her close resemblance to the more recent of his wives, and the thought that she had ceased to be a menace was very comforting.

He had been musing thus for some little time, when the sound of the front-door bell broke in on his reverie. He rose and went to answer it. Doing so, he recognized, involved a risk, but it had to be taken, for it might be his friend Trout who had rung. He was particularly anxious to see Trout. Trout would support his view that in his dealings with Vera Dalrymple he was proceeding on the right lines; and however confident he may be that he has outgeneralled a woman, a man likes to have reassurance on the point from a knowledgeable third party.

It was his friend Trout, but a very different Trout from the Trout of the previous night; a Trout glowing from head to foot and quite capable of doing buck-and-wing dances on the door-mat. Even in repose he seemed on the verge of one of those soft-shoe Shuffle-off-to-Buffalo forms of self-expression which used to be so popular in American vaudeville. He twitched, and his feet pawed the carpet like those of some mettlesome steed.

These phenomena passed unnoticed by Mr Llewellyn. It is never easy to detect molten passion from outside, particularly if you are rather self-centred, as he was. Trout to him, whether a-glow or with his inner light turned off, was just Trout. He said he was glad to see him and hoped that he could dine with him, and Mr Trout said he already had a dinner date. Sherlock Holmes, had he been present, would have drawn conclusions from the tremor in his voice as he spoke, but it made no impression on Mr Llewellyn. If he thought anything about it, he merely assumed that Mr Trout was suffering from catarrh.

'I can only stop a minute,' said Mr Trout. 'I'm on my way to get my hair trimmed. I just looked in to have a word with young Pickering.'

'What about?'

'Oh, just something I have to tell him. Nice boy, Pickering. We spent the afternoon together.'

'Doing what?'

'Chasing girls in taxi cabs.'

'I thought you didn't go in for that sort of thing.'

'As a rule no, but Pickering made a point of it.'

'Damn fool. Playing with fire.'

'Would you say that?'

'Yes, I would say that. If that's the way he's going to carry on, he'll be married before he knows what's hit him.'

Mr Trout forbore to comment on this sentiment. Lawyers learn to be diplomatic, and he could see that the subject had begun to annoy his friend.

'You didn't tell me if Pickering was in,' he said.

'No, he went out for a walk, looking like a rainy Sunday in Pittsburgh. Why he was looking like that he didn't explain.'

'It's his love life, I.L. It's come a stinker.'

'He doesn't know his luck.'

A spasm of pain passed over Mr Trout's face, as if he had been a curate compelled to listen to blasphemy from his vicar. Pursuing his policy of being diplomatic, he said nothing on the subject but in between two dance steps asked if Mr Llewellyn happened to know the name of the girl to whom Joe Pickering had given his heart.

'Sure,' said Mr Llewellyn. 'She interviewed me for her paper. It's Fitch. Did you ever hear a song of Cole Porter's – "Mister and Mrs Fitch"?'

'No.'

'Good song. I often sing it in my bath.'

'Indeed? I would like to hear it.'

'You must drop in some morning. About half-past nine would be the best time. Bring a raincoat, as I splash about a good deal. It's one of those songs that need putting over with gestures.'

Mr Llewellyn paused. Mr Trout had begun to float about the room like something out of Swan Lake, and Mr Llewellyn disapproved of this. He was apt to be a martinet in his dealings with his legal advisers, demanding that lawyers should behave like lawyers and leave eccentric dancing to the professionals. A man, he held, is either Fred Astaire or he is not Fred Astaire, and if he is not Fred Astaire he should not carry on like him. For the first time it struck him that there was an oddness in Mr Trout this evening, as if he on honeydew had fed and drunk the milk of Paradise, and he did not pay him a substantial annual retainer for doing that.

There was abruptness in his voice as he said:

'Why do you want the girl's name?'

'I shall be calling on her shortly, and I'd like to know who to ask for. She lives, I understand, at Fountain Court, Park Lane. It is my intention to see her and effect a reconciliation between

95

her and Pickering. I don't like the thought of two loving hearts being parted by a misunderstanding. Who do you think I am? Thomas Hardy?'

Mr Llewellyn was now definitely perplexed. He could make nothing of this. Mr Trout's diction was beautifully clear, leaving no possibility that he could have mistaken what he said, but his words did not appear to make sense. He would have scorched him with a rebuking glare if Mr Trout had stayed still long enough for it to reach its target, but had to content himself with projecting a rebuking glare in his general direction.

'Trout,' he said, 'have you had a couple?'

'Certainly not.'

'Then why are you talking this apple sauce about loving hearts? Last night –'

He did not complete the sentence. The telephone was ringing.

'Answer that, Trout,' said Mr Llewellyn. 'If it's for me, say I'm out.'

Mr Trout went to the instrument, and the first words he uttered caused Mr Llewellyn to stiffen from head to foot like a nymph surprised while bathing, for they were 'Good evening, madam', and they froze him to the marrow. Warmly he congratulated himself on his prudence in telling Mr Trout to answer the call. London, of course, was full of those who might be addressed as 'Madam', but he could think of only one. To only one, moreover, he had given his telephone number. He feared the worst. It appalled him to think how nearly he had come to kidding back and forth with Vera Dalrymple, a course which could not but have ended in disaster. He waited breathlessly for Mr Trout to say he was out.

'I am afraid,' said Mr Trout in his polished manner, 'that he is not at home at the moment, but he should be returning shortly, and I will not fail to give him your message. I am sure he will be delighted. Not at all,' said Mr Trout, apparently in answer to some expression of thanks at the other end. 'A pleasure. Goodbye, madam, goodbye. What lovely weather we are having, are we not? A Miss Dalrymple,' he said, hanging up. 'She wants you to give her dinner the day after tomorrow. She will be calling for you at about seven-thirty.'

Mr Llewellyn was staring dumbly, as Tennyson's Lady of Shalott might have stared when the mirror cracked from side to side and the curse had come upon her. Indeed, if the Lady of Shalott had entered at this moment, he would have slapped her on the back and told her he knew just how she felt.

'And ... you ... told ... her ... you ... were ... sure ... I ... would ... be ... delighted!' he whispered.

Having said this, he was silent for a space, wrestling with his feelings. He was wondering how he had ever looked on Ephraim Trout as a friend and resolving, as soon as he could get around to it, to transfer his legal affairs from his hands and place them in those of Jones, Jukes, Jerningham and Jenkinson. Would Jones, he reasoned, have told Vera Dalrymple that he would be delighted to give her dinner? Would Jukes? Not a chance. Nor would Jenkinson and Jerningham. And this was a man who prided himself on belonging to Bachelors Anonymous. It was enough to make one ask oneself what things were coming to. It is not too much to say that Mr Llewellyn was stricken to the core.

Men who are stricken to the core react in one of two ways. They rave and curse – this was the method preferred by King Lear – all that Blow, winds, and crack your cheeks stuff – or a sort of frozen calm comes over them as if their circulation had been suspended. It was to the latter school that Mr Llewellyn belonged. He might become irritable over trifles, but in serious crises he was a block of ice. On the occasion when Weinstein-Colossal had stolen two of his best stars nobody could have guessed from his demeanour the volcanic fury that was surging within him. So now he said almost gently:

'You told her I would be delighted, did you? Do you realize that if I give this woman dinner, I shall almost certainly ask her to marry me?'

'And you couldn't do better,' said Mr Trout heartily. 'I have not had the pleasure of meeting her, but I assume that she is charming, and the thing that matters is to get married. Who was it described bachelors as wild asses of the desert? I forget, but he was right, and what future is there for a wild ass? Practically none. It just goes on being a wild ass until something happens to end its aimless existence, and nobody cares a damn when it's gone. You're crazy if you intend to go on being a lonely bachelor, not that I suppose one could actually call you a bachelor. Marriage is the only road to contentment and happiness. Think of the quiet home evenings, she busy knitting the tiny garments, you in the old armchair with your crossword puzzle. Think of the companionship, the feeling that you are never going to be alone again. Get married, I.L. Give this Dalrymple dinner tomorrow and over the meal attach yourself to her little hand and ask her to be yours. Excuse me,' said Mr Trout. 'I must be going. I have to get a shampoo and manicure in addition to the hair-trim.'

The effect of this eloquence on Mr Llewellyn was to add to the emotions of the Lady of Shalott those of Julius Caesar when stabbed by Brutus. We can put up with the knavish tricks of enemies – we may not like them, but we can endure them – but when we are betrayed by a friend we drain the bitter cup and no heel taps. The one thing Mr Llewellyn had been sure he could rely on was the stability of the Trout doctrine. Whoever else might fail him, Trout was a solid rock. And here he was, mouthing these dreadful sentiments without, apparently, a qualm. He could not have been more horrified and in the depths if he had been a Tory member of Parliament and had heard his leader expressing the opinion that there was a lot of sound sense in the works of Karl Marx, and the Communists were not such bad chaps if you got to know them.

We have said that in moments of crisis Mr Llewellyn always preserved an outward calm, but that was intended to apply only to ordinary crises. In one of this magnitude he could not be expected to keep dismay from showing in his appearance. When Mr Trout had left him, his tredipation was unmistakable. He sat motionless in his chair, looking like something the cat had brought in. Even such a man, so faint, so spiritless, so dull, so dead in look, so woebegone, drew Priam's curtain at the dead of night and would have told him half his Troy was burned.

It was thus that Joe, returning from his walk, found him, and it is greatly to his credit that one glance at that haggard face told him that his own troubles must be shelved for the time being and all his faculties concentrated on those of his employer.

'Good Lord,' he said. 'What's the matter?'

In broken accents Mr Llewellyn started to fill him in, as he would have put it, but the accents were not so broken as to render Joe incapable of following the scenario. Having the advantage of knowing Miss Dalrymple, he was able to appreciate without difficulty the emotions of anyone who found himself in danger of marrying her, and he would have clasped Mr Llewellyn's hand, had not the latter been waving it. Very clearly he saw that now was the time for all good men to come to the aid of the party.

'I don't like this,' he said.

'Well, you don't suppose *I* do,' said Mr Llewellyn.

'But what I don't understand is why you have to ask her to marry you. Surely there are other things you can talk about at dinner. The weather, books, the situation in China, the prospects of a general election.'

Mr Llewellyn uttered an impatient snort.

'I explained that to you very clearly the day we met, but I see that I shall have to do it again. The first thing you have to grasp is that I am a man of intense sensitiveness and spirituality. Got that into your nut? I can't hurt people's feelings. Do you understand that, or are you as big a damned fool as you look? Well then, I take her to dinner. At first everything's all right. We get through the soup, fish and whatever it may be without disaster because she's biding her time, and then we come to the coffee. Coffee's the danger spot. There is a pause in the conversation.'

'Why?'

'Because she's preparing to unmask her batteries. She is sitting with a sort of faraway look on her face. She heaves a sigh. She says what a lonely life hers is and how hollow success is and how the applause of her public can never make up for not having a home. Upon which, I ask her to marry me. It's something to say. It's put me off coffee for life. All my marriages came about like that, even Bernadine Friganza, who wouldn't have recognized a home if you had brought her one on a plate with watercress around it.'

'And they never refuse you?'

'Of course not. Who would?'

Joe pondered. What with his sensitiveness and spirituality this man was plainly an object for concern. He could see but one solution of his problem.

'You mustn't take Vera Dalrymple to dinner.'

'How can I get out of it? She's calling for me the day after tomorrow at seven-thirty.'

'You mustn't be here.'

'Where else can I be?'

'In hospital.'

'In *what*?'

'Hospital. You'll be safe there.'

Again Mr Llewellyn snorted. If Joe had been making a suggestion at a studio conference, he could not have snorted more vehemently.

'And how do I get into a hospital? What do you propose that I shall do? Get run over by a taxi cab? Chew soap and pretend I'm having a fit?'

'Tell them you want a check-up. You probably need one anyway.'

Ths fire faded from Mr Llewellyn's eyes. The snort was silent on his lips. He regarded Joe with the admiration of a fond father whose infant son has spoken his first word.

'Pickering,' he said, 'I believe you've got something. She couldn't get at me in hospital.'

'Only on visiting days.'

'Between stated hours.'

'With nurses coming in and out all the time.'

'Exactly.'

'Watch out for the grapes, of course.'

'I don't get you.'

'She will bring you grapes. You don't want them to lead to anything.'

'I'll tell the doctor my doctor has forbidden them.'

'Because you're subject to appendicitis.'

'Exactly. Pickering, you're a marvel.'

'Awfully nice of you to say so.'

'And do you know what I'm going to do?'

'Keep off the grapes.'

'That of course, but in addition I'm going to make a picture of that play of yours. That's what I'm going to do. Presence of mind like yours deserves a rich reward.'

Chapter Eleven

In accents as broken as those of Mr Llewellyn – on these emotional occasions it is rarely that an accent escapes unbroken – Joe expressed his gratitude and gratification, and Mr Llewellyn repeated the statement he had made at their first meeting, that *Cousin Angela*, while he did not expect it to be great or even colossal, would make a good picture. It would, he pointed out, not be handicapped, as the play had been, by having Vera Dalrymple in it. Miss Dalrymple, he said, had dropped several hints that she was open to consider a Hollywood contract, but, he added, any time he let loose that sinister menace in the neighbourhood of Beverly Hills you could write him down as one who needed to have his head examined.

'And now to pack,' he said.

'Pack?' said Joe.

'A few necessaries – toothbrush, razor, shaving cream, pyjamas and a couple of Agatha Christies. I'm off to hospital.'

'But you can't just walk into a hospital. You have to be sent there by a doctor.'

'Where did you hear that?'

'Everybody knows it.'

'I didn't,' said Mr Llewellyn discontentedly. 'Do you mean I won't be able to get in till tomorrow? Then I'll have to go to a hotel for the night. I'm not going to stay here wondering when Vera Dalrymple will ring that front-door bell. I wouldn't sleep a wink.'

'She said she wasn't coming till the day after tomorrow.'

'Just her subtle cunning. Lulling me into a false security.'

It was with mixed feelings that Joe escorted his benefactor to the door. At one moment the realization that the waving of Mr Llewellyn's magic wand was about to place him in the sound financial position of which he had so often dreamed elated him;

at the next he was cast into the depths by the thought that, however much money he made from the motion picture sale of *Cousin Angela*, the odds on his being able to share it with the girl he loved could scarcely be quoted at better than a hundred to eight. Indeed, taking into consideration her policy of refusing to speak to him, a shrewd turf accountant would probably make them even longer.

Sally's behaviour bewildered him. He could understand his non-appearance at the dinner table causing a certain annoyance, but the fact of her not giving him a chance to explain was beyond his comprehension. It piqued him, too, that such a splendid explanation should be going to waste. If there is one excuse for failing to keep a tryst that is beyond the reach of criticism, it is surely sudden illness.

That sudden illness perplexed Joe. His health had always been perfect, never more so than when Mr Trout was handing him the beaker. The reflection that in next to no time he would be seated opposite Sally in Barribault's grill room, with the lights down low and the fiddler of whom Mr Llewellyn disapproved so much straining at the leash and all ready to give of his best, had sent a shiver down his spine and filled him with what the French in their peculiar way call *bien être*. An unfortunate moment to be struck by lightning, as he apparently had been.

It was very quiet in the flat, and it was not long before the silence began to prey on Joe's nerves. A man whose spirits are as low as his yearns for companionship. A dog, even a dog like Mrs Bingham's Percy, might have helped, but 8 Enniston Gardens contained no dog. In a sudden flash of inspiration Joe thought of Jerry Nichols.

It was in not too sanguine a frame of mind that he went to the telephone and dialled his number. If Jerry had a defect, it was that his attitude towards the other sex was frivolous. He was not one of the Joe Pickerings, whose hearts when once bestowed are given for ever. He was one of those volatile young men who take on a wide field in the way of female society, and was apt to count that day lost when he did not entertain what he described as a popsy at the evening meal. The cocktail hour being now imminent, it was more than probable that his time would be spoken for.

And so it proved. In answer to Joe's invitation he was compelled to proclaim himself unavailable.

'Sorry, Joe. I've got a date.'

'Can't you put her off?'

'It isn't a her, it's Father. He likes me to hob-nob with him once in a while, and tonight happens to be the while it's a once in.'

'Oh, hell.'

'Why the dismay? Surely you can do without me for one night. Clench the teeth. It only needs willpower.'

'I want your advice about something.'

'Oh, that's different. I'm always eager to give advice. I'll tell you what I'll do. Father always goes to sleep after feeding owing to plentiful doses of old port and he dines on the stroke of dusk. I'll steal away and come and see you.'

Joe returned to his solitary brooding. He was soon obsessed with the idea that only through Jerry could his problem be solved. After all, he felt, a man so given to mingling with popsies must often have come up against a problem similar to his and would have been taught by experience how to handle it. By the time Mr Trout arrived Joe's mental attitude towards Jerry had become that of a disciple towards a sage or seer.

The advent of Mr Trout came on him as a surprise. He had not been warned that he would be calling, and he was not at all sure that he was glad to see him. He would have welcomed him with more pleasure if there had been in his demeanour a decent melancholy, for in his current mood the last thing he wanted to see about him was smiling faces, and a single glance told him that here was somebody who was sitting on a pink cloud with a rainbow round his shoulder. Mr Trout had not yet burst into song with a hey-nonny-nonny and a hot-cha-cha, but when you said that you had said everything.

'Oh, hullo,' he mumbled.

'Good evening, good evening, good evening,' said Mr Trout. He might have been one of a comedy duo billed as The Sunshine Boys, good dressers on and off. 'How lovely the world looks in the gloaming. London becomes a veritable fairyland. One is reminded of the words of the poet, which I have forgotten at the moment, but they are very beautiful. Is Llewellyn in?'

'No, he went out.'

'All for the best. I'm glad. Because I want to talk to you privately, Pickering. In the cab this afternoon I let fall some observations on the subject of love and marriage which I now regret.'

'Oh, did you?'

'I did, though apparently you were not listening. I expressed myself very strongly as disapproving of them. My views have since become radically altered. I am now wholeheartedly in their favour. It is love that makes the world go round, I am now convinced. I remember a song, popular many years ago, entitled "Love me and the world is mine". That's the spirit, Pickering, that's the spirit. An admirable sentiment.'

Joe was looking at him with a wild surmise. Had his diction not been so clear and his lower limbs so firm, he would, like Mr Llewellyn, have entertained doubts of his sobriety. As it was, he merely gaped, hoping that footnotes would be supplied later.

'Well, that's fine,' he said.

'"Fine" is the word, Pickering.'

'But you were saying that you had something private to talk to me about.'

'And I have, I have indeed. But in order to make my story intelligible to you I shall have to give an account of my life up to this afternoon. A brief account,' he added, seeing Joe wince. 'Just an outline.'

'Omitting childhood, boyhood and college days?'

'Precisely. The periods you mention are not of the essence. We move directly to my mature manhood.'

'That's good.'

'When I became a member of Bachelors Anonymous.'

'Alcoholics Anonymous?'

'*Bachelors* Anonymous. A little group of men whose aim in life it is to avoid getting married. We strain every nerve to preserve our celibacy, and if we hear of a fellow-member weakening, we plead with him to be strong. We even have a song which we sing on these occasions. "Of all the ills with which we're cursed the married state is far the worst", it begins. I could sing it to you, if you wish.'

'Some other time, do you think?'

'Any time that suits you. It's a catchy little thing.'

'I'll bet.'

'Lyric by Johnny Runcible, music by G. J. Flannery.'

Joe stirred uneasily. Mr Trout had not given any formal promise not to sing, and there was no knowing when he might not do it. He shrank from having to listen on an empty stomach. To divert his companion's attention and prevent this becoming a musical evening he put a question.

'Has all this anything to do with me? It's all absorbingly interesting, but where do I come in?'

'I am about to tell you. But first I must reveal that I am no longer a member of Bachelors Anonymous. I cabled my resignation on my way here. I am afraid the boys will be terribly upset, but I had no option. As I told you, my views have undergone a radical change. It happened down at Valley Fields this afternoon. It was there that love found me, Pickering. I met a woman who taught me the meaning of passion.'

Joe's bewilderment increased. He could think of but one female resident of Valley Fields.

'Not the woman with the X-ray eyes who talked about fleshy lusts and told me the Kingdom of Heaven was at hand?'

'I was too far off to hear what she told you, and in addition the cabman was telling me how wet weather always brings on his lumbago. But no, she was not the one. The divine creature to whom I allude is a Mrs Amelia Bingham who lives next door.'

Joe pursed his lips. He was shocked.

'*Mrs?* Trout,' he said severely, 'are you breaking up a home?'

'No, no, no, no, no.'

'Are you a modern Casanova?'

'Certainly not. Mrs Bingham is a widow. Her late husband fell overboard on a day excursion to Boulogne.'

There was a momentary silence while their thoughts dwelled on Mr Bingham, deceased.

'She bakes the most wonderful scones,' said Mr Trout.

'Oh?' said Joe.

'And her strawberry jam has to be tasted to be believed.'

'Oh?'

'You will notice that I have a bandage on my hand. Her dog bit me and she bound me up.'

'Oh?'

'With extraordinary skill. She is a hospital nurse.'

Joe rose once more to a point of order.

'All this may be so, but I don't see where I get into the act.'

'I beg your pardon?'

'What has all this got to do with me?'

'I am coming to that. I have merely been laying the foundation for my apology. What we call in the Law connecting up. If I had never met Mrs Bingham and ceased to be a member of Bachelors Anonymous, I should not have felt compelled to apologize to you.'

'What's all this about apologizing? Apologizing for what?'

'For putting that Mickey Finn in your highball yesterday.'

In one of her early novels Rosie M. Banks has a passage in which she described the reaction of Claude Delamere, the hero, on becoming aware that the girl to whom he was betrothed had not, as he had supposed, been deceiving him. (It was her brother from Australia he had seen her kissing.) He felt, she says, as if a blinding light had flashed upon him. It was much the same with Joe Pickering as he heard these words. But whereas Claude had been filled with a joy that threatened to unman him, he was as sore as a sunburned neck and as mad as a hornet. So intense was his righteous wrath that he could not speak, merely standing there making a noise like the death rattle of an expiring soda syphon, and Mr Trout proceeded.

'Yes, I do feel I owe you an apology, though I must claim to have had some excuse for acting as I did. You had spoken of the girl with the utmost enthusiasm, you were taking her to dinner, you had had a manicure and a shampoo. Naturally it seemed to a lifelong member of Bachelors Anonymous that there was no time to be lost and that only Method B would serve. I was actuated by motives of the purest altruism. I felt I had a mission to save you from yourself. I pictured you thanking me later with tears in your eyes. How could I know that I was going to meet Mrs Bingham and see the light? I can only say I'm sorry. But as a matter of fact no harm has been done. All you have to do is go to the girl and explain. You will probably have a good laugh together. Bless my soul,' said Mr Trout, looking at his watch. 'Is that the time? I must rush.' And he was gone.

But any shortage of Trouts was compensated for an hour later by the arrival of Jerry Nichols, who announced that his father had fallen asleep much more promptly than usual, thus enabling him to be at Joe's service with the minimum of delay.

'What seems to be the trouble?' he asked.

It did not take Joe long to inform him. The basic facts were readily tabulated. He loved a girl, and she would not speak to him. Jerry agreed that this was a disagreeable state of affairs.

'Who is this girl?'

'Sally Fitch. You've met her. She came to see you that day I was in your office about the Llewellyn job.'

'Oh, the heiress.'

'The what?'

'We had asked her to call because somebody had left her twenty-five thousand pounds.'

'What!'

'Didn't you know?'

'Of course I didn't. Good Lord, Jerry, do you think she thinks I do know and am after her for her money?'

'Impossible. Any girl with an ounce of sense could see that you aren't that sort of chap. Rugged honesty, that's you. It sticks out all over you. No, it must be something you've done. Have you done something?'

'Yes, but I can explain.'

'Tell me all.'

'I asked her to dinner and didn't show up. Naturally this would have annoyed her, but you'd think she would let me explain. But she won't.'

'Your explanation being – ?'

'That just as I was starting out for the restaurant somebody gave me a Mickey Finn.'

'Somebody what?'

'Gave me a Mickey Finn. You know what a Mickey Finn is?'

A rather careworn look had come into Jerry's face. It was plain that he was having difficulty in becoming equal to the intellectual pressure of the conversation.

'I think you had better tell me the Pickering Story from the beginning, Joe. At the moment a bit abstruse it strikes me as.'

Joe told it to him from the beginning, and Jerry listened with growing understanding.

'You're quite right,' he said at its conclusion. 'You can certainly explain. I don't mind telling you that there have been times in my life when I've wished I had as good an explanation as that. We must call on this Fitch first thing tomorrow.'

'But she won't see me.'

'She'll see you all right. The lay-out is as follows. We go to her address, we ring the bell, the door is opened and we slide in, and there we are. I say "we" because I shall be at your side. You then tell her about the Mickey Finn. Good?'

'Perfect.'

'Not so good,' said Jerry. 'Because on seeing you crossing the threshold she would break into a spring and go and lock herself in the bathroom. Obviously you mustn't be there. I will go and see her and report to you if the All Clear has been blown. I say "if", for we must never lose sight of the fact that the explanation of yours takes a lot of believing. It needs someone like myself to put it over.'

Chapter Twelve

At times when one's affairs have become tangled, causing the brow to develop furrows and the soul to ask itself 'Where do we go from here?', it is always a comfort to place oneself in the hands of a recognized expert and allow him to carry on. Householders feel a new hope when something has gone wrong with the pipes and the plumber arrives, and the thought that Jerry, a man accustomed to coping with popsies since he was a slip of a boy, had taken over the difficult negotiations with Sally brought a new hope to Joe Pickering. It was in quite cheerful mood that he rose from the breakfast table next morning to answer the telephone. Before he had enlisted Jerry's aid his 'Hullo?' would have been a low faint 'Hullo?', almost a gurgle. Now it had quite a ring.

'Hoy!' said the telephone. 'Pickering?'

'Oh hullo, Mr Llewellyn. Are you in the hospital?'

'Sure I'm in the hospital. St Swithin's.'

'Everything all right?'

'More or less. Hell of a lot of noise going on all the time. There's a contraption outside my room which keeps bellowing "Doctor Binns, Doctor Binns" every two minutes. What it wants Doctor Binns for I don't know. Probably to tell him a funny story. But that's not what I called up about. It suddenly occurred to me that the man Trout might come and ask you where I was. On no account tell him. The first thing he would do would be to run bleating to the Dalrymple pot of poison and spill the beans, and half an hour after that she would be round here with grapes and kind inquiries.'

'But he doesn't know where she lives.'

'He would find out. A man like Trout can find out anything. So don't breathe a word.'

'My lips are sealed.'

'Your hips are what?'

'Not hips, lips. I said they were sealed.'

'Keep them that way.'

A brief pause in the conversation took place at this point. A confused roaring noise, as of lions at feeding time, came over the wire. Then Mr Llewellyn spoke again.

'Pickering.'

'On the spot.'

'That was a girl in short skirts and a white thungummy on the back of her head who wanted a sample of my blood. I very soon told her where she got off. "I don't give samples of my blood to every Tom Dick and Harry who comes asking for them," I said.'

'Only to personal friends?'

'Exactly. She didn't know which way to look. What were we talking about?'

'Mr Trout.'

'Don't call him Mister Trout. The hellhound Trout or Trout the traitor, if you like, but not a term of respect like Mister. Personally, it gives me a sinking feeling even to think of him. Ever hear of Benedict Arnold?'

'I've read about him.'

'Trout's name ought to have been that.'

'Don't you mean his name ought to have been Trout?'

'Do I?'

'I think so.'

'Perhaps you're right. But why you want to keep babbling on about a human gumboil like Trout I can't imagine.'

'Sorry.'

'What?'

'I said I was sorry.'

'Then don't do it again.'

'I won't. How do you like it in hospital?'

'Might be worse. All right for a visit, but I wouldn't live there if you gave me the place.'

'Nice nurse?'

'Ah, there you have said a mouthful, Pickering. I have a Grade A nurse.'

'Splendid.'

'The very word for her. Not one of your juvenile delinquents who bust in on you wanting samples of your blood, but a sensible comfortable middle-aged woman in her forties. We get on like a couple of sailors on shore leave. Well, go to hell now, Pickering; I'm expecting the doctor. Remember about Benedict Arnold Trout.'

'I won't forget.'

'Not a word if he comes inquiring as to my whereabouts.'

An old joke about them being at the wash flitted into Joe's mind, but he let it go. He was feeling better than he had been feeling, but not so much better as to allow him to indulge in light persiflage of that nature.

The upward trend in his spirits did not last. Despondency returned and grew, for the afternoon, though bringing callers of various descriptions including an optimist who hoped to sell richly bound and illustrated sets of Dumas on the easy payment system, did not bring Jerry Nichols. The evening was well advanced before he appeared.

'Well, you've taken your time,' said Joe.

Jerry dismissed the slur with a wave of the hand not unlike one of Mr Llewellyn's gestures when singing 'Mister and Mrs Fitch' in his bath.

'I came as soon as I could,' he said. 'I would have thought that you, being in the same line of business yourself until recently, would have been familiar with the iron discipline which prevails in a solicitor's office. If Father had caught me sneaking off before closing time, it would have made no difference that I was his son, I would have been marched off into a hollow square of clerks and office boys and had my buttons snipped off, or probably something even worse. You remember what happened to Danny Deever in the morning.'

Joe had to admit the justice of this. The head of Nichols, Trubshaw and Nichols might take a nap after dinner now and then, but in the daytime his vigilance would have been that of the keenest-eyed type of lynx. He apologized, and Jerry begged him not to mention it. He was accustomed to being misjudged, he said. He would now, he added, proceed to make his report, a statement which brought Joe up in his chair as if a sharp instrument had come through its seat.

'Did you see her?'

'No.'

'Why not?'

'She wasn't there. A girl doesn't stay indoors all day. She has things to do which take her out from time to time. Let me tell you the whole story, omitting no detail however slight. I got to Fountain Court and rang the bell. All straight so far?' he said rather unnecessarily, and Joe said he had found no difficulty in following the narrative up to this point. Seeming pleased with his intelligence, Jerry resumed.

'The door was opened by a rather personable popsy, who proved to be a girl who lives with the Fitch. She informed me that the Fitch was at the hair stylist's having a permanent. "You had better look in later," she said. "There's a man called Trout waiting to see her." Well, I wasn't going to have that, of course. "Later be blowed," I said. "I have to see Miss Fitch on a matter of the utmost urgency, the nature of which I am not empowered to divulge. I'm jolly well coming in, and if Trout objects, I'll scatter him to the four winds." "Suit yourself," she said. "It's a free country," and she buzzed off, and I went on into the living-room where, as foreshadowed, I found Trout.'

'Trout,' said Joe meditatively.

'That was the name.'

'I wonder what he wanted.'

'He told me that. His mission was the same as mine. He had come to tell Miss Fitch that he was the bloke who had given you that Mickey Finn which had caused your non-appearance at the dinner table.'

'My God!'

'Precisely. With your quick intelligence you have spotted that the coming clean of Trout is the one thing that was needed to extricate you from the soup in which you are wallowing. It gives verisimilitude to an otherwise bald and unconvincing narrative. I go to her and say "Hullo there, Miss Fitch, I'll bet you've been wondering why Joe asked you to dinner and didn't turn up. The matter is readily explained. Somebody gave him a Mickey Finn", and it carries little or no conviction. But it's very different when Trout, tapping his chest, says "*I dun it.*" She swallows his story whole and asks for more.'

'Of course!'

'It's what we lawyers call the best evidence. The other sort is incompetent, irrelevant and immaterial and doesn't get you anywhere. I decided, accordingly, to come away and leave it to Trout to do the talking, though sorry not to see Miss Fitch again, for she had impressed me very favourably that time she came to my office. Nice girl.'

'How long does a permanent take?'

'I don't know. I've never had one. But I see what's in your mind. You're wondering if she'll be back by now. Probably, I should think.'

'Then I'll be moving along. And thanks for all you've done, Jerry.'

'A pleasure, old man, a pleasure. Not that I've done much. But, as I often say, it's the Boy Scout spirit that counts. Oh, one last word, Have you given any thought to what happens when you and she meet?'

'We talk things over, I suppose.'

'Talk things over be blowed. Don't waste time chatting. Get immediate action. Skip the red tape. Grab her, fold her in a close embrace and hug her till her ribs squeak. I have tried this policy on several occasions, and I have always found it to give the best results.'

2

London looked very beautiful to Joe as he drove to Fountain Court. Mr Trout had described it as a veritable fairyland, and he had been, Joe thought, pretty accurate. The streets were full of delightful-looking people with whom he was sure he would have got on splendidly if he had only had time to stop and fraternize. The dogs, too, taking the air on leashes. He would have liked, had speed not been so important, to have got out and passed the time of day with all of them and with the cats as well, if there had been any. He was, in a word, feeling in mid-season form and getting more so every minute.

As he drove, he mused on Mr Trout, and thought what a capital fellow he was. If that was the sort of man California produced, one could understand it being known as the Jewel State of the Union. A purist might shake his head at the old gentleman's practice of introducing foreign substances into people's drinks, but that was a negligible flaw in an otherwise saintly character, and how superbly he made amends when he considered the time had come for making them. Remorse gripped Joe as he thought how churlishly he had denied Mr Trout the pleasure of telling him all about his childhood, boyhood and college days and singing him the Bachelors Anonymous theme song.

It was Mr Trout who opened the door of 3A Fountain Court to him. One might have supposed that, having said his say, he would have left the premises, but Mr Trout was one of those men who do not leave premises. They stay on, waiting to see what is going to happen next.

They conversed in the hall.

'You've told her?' said Joe urgently.

Mr Trout said he had, and might have added that Joe could have guessed as much from his beaming countenance.

Pausing only to say 'At-a-boy', Joe asked how she had taken it.

'She wept.'

'*Wept?*'

'Tears of joy. She was overjoyed, Pickering. It was obvious that a great weight had been lifted from her mind and that the sun had –'

'Come smiling through?'

'The very phrase I was about to employ. It made me feel very happy, Pickering, to think that I had been instrumental in joining two sundered hearts together. Strange how one's views can change, as it were in a flash. It seems only yesterday, in fact it was only yesterday, that I thought the great thing with sundered hearts was to keep them sundered.'

'So you think everything's all right?'

'Everything is perfect. True, she is engaged to be married to somebody else, but she is extremely fond of you. It showed clearly in her manner.'

The effect of these words on Joe was somewhat similar to that which would have been produced by a blow on the bridge of the nose by a wet fish. His jaw fell. His eyes bulged. He tottered and might have fallen had he not clutched at the umbrella stand.

'Engaged to someone else?' he quavered.

'Yes. Owing, I gathered, to a regrettable misunderstanding. You asked her to lunch, and she was prevented by circumstances over which she had no control from putting in an appearance. When subsequently you asked her to dinner and in your turn did not put in an appearance, she assumed that you had done it to punish her, and being a girl of spirit she resented it. So when this man asked her to marry him, she accepted him by way of evening the score. The whole affair has in it something of the inevitability of Greek tragedy.'

'And it wouldn't have happened,' said Joe bitterly, removing a hand from the umbrella stand and waving it, 'if you didn't go about the place giving people Mickey Finns.'

A faint blush mantled Mr Trout's cheek.

'Yes,' he said, 'I suppose that is in a measure true. But you must remember that I thought I was acting in your best interests. And fortunately no harm has been done.'

'No harm?'

'I am convinced that you have only to fold her in a close embrace and she will forget all about this other man to whom she has rashly become affianced. Those tears of joy told the story. Fold her in a close embrace, and all will be well.'

Joe was impressed. Had this advice come solely from Mr Trout, he might have ignored it, reasoning that a veteran member of Bachelors Anonymous could scarcely be accepted as a fount of wisdom where feminine psychology was concerned. But Jerry Nichols had said the same thing, and Jerry was a man who knew. Any theory promulgated by him must have been tested a dozen times and proved correct.

The strong-arm methods favoured by both counsellors might,

116

of course, be resented, for he had no official knowledge that his love was returned. Nevertheless, he was resolved to put his fate to the touch to win or to lose it all, as recommended by the poet Montrose. The phrase 'Nothing venture, nothing have' occurred to him. At the worst, if she drew herself to her full height and said 'Sir!' he would have kissed her and would have that memory to cheer him up in the long lonely winter evenings. Even if given time for only two or three kisses, he would be that much ahead of the game.

'Is she in there?' he said, indicating the door of the sitting-room.

'No,' said Mr Trout. 'When I had told my story, she went off in a cab.'

'What on earth for?'

'To see you, of course. Little knowing that you were on your way to see *her*. Quite an amusing little mix-up,' said Mr Trout.

And as he spoke a key clicked in the door.

3

A key clicking in a door is one of London's smaller sounds, not to be compared for volume to the thousand others which enliven life in that city, but the click of this one could not have arrested Joe's attention more immediately if it had been the explosion of a bomb. He quivered in every limb, and when the door opened and Sally entered he was about to leap forward and fold her in a close embrace, when she leaped forward and folded *him* in one, at the same time saying 'Oh, Joe, Joe, Joe!' It was plain that she, like Jerry, believed in skipping red tape and proceeding at once to the direct action which speaks so much louder than words.

'Oh, Joe!' said Sally.

'Oh, Sally!' said Joe.

'I've been feeling awful,' said Sally.

'Me, too,' said Joe. 'I wish I had a quid for every time I've thought of sticking my head in the gas oven.'

'Oh, Joe!' said Sally.

'Oh, Sally!' said Joe.

A man of more delicacy than Mr Trout would have withdrawn softly at this point, feeling that the tender scene was one that did not demand the presence of an audience, but Mr Trout's slowness at leaving premises was equalled by his reluctance to withdraw from tender scenes. He stood there drinking in this one with a benevolent smile.

It was a smile which conveyed only benevolence, but there was in his eyes anxiety and concern, for he was feeling that everything was not so simple as the two principals appeared to think. And when he heard Joe speaking enthusiastically of visits to registry offices and Sally falling in eagerly with the suggestion, he called attention to himself with one of those dry coughs in which lawyers specialize.

'Are we not forgetting something?' he said.

Joe started violently. He had had no notion that Mr Trout was among those present. He had supposed that on seeing Sally he would have realized that his company was not desired. But, as had been shown, it would have come as a surprise to him to learn that his company was ever not desired. He was as difficult to dislodge as a family spectre.

'Good Lord!' said Joe. 'Are you still here?'

'Still here,' Mr Trout assured him. 'And when you speak of immediate visits to registry offices with Miss Fitch, I think it is only fitting to remind you that she is engaged to be married to someone else.'

He had anticipated that the point he was raising would have a damping effect, and he was right. It did have a damping effect. Joe blinked and released Sally, and Sally collapsed on the umbrella stand.

'Who is this fellow you're engaged to?' Joe demanded.

'Jaklyn Warner,' said Sally, and Joe had to rebuke her.

'No, this is serious, darling,' he said. 'Don't cloud the issue by being funny. Who are you really engaged to?'

'Jaklyn Warner.'

'But you can't be. You've never met him.'

'I've known him for years.'

'Then you must realize the utter impossibility of marrying him.'

'Who is this Mr Warner?' asked Mr Trout. 'Eh? Oh, I was not aware. Who is this Sir Jaklyn Warner?'

It was a question which Joe felt fully competent to answer.

'He is London's leading louse, a worm, a chiseller, a rat, a sponger, never done a stroke of work in his life, supports himself by borrowing money, which of course he never pays back.'

Mr Trout nodded sagely.

'I know the type. Young men like that abound in Hollywood. They live on cocktails and appetizers at parties to which they have not been invited. They roam the streets of Beverly Hills till they hear music and see a string of coloured lanterns, and then they go in and eat sausages on little sticks. I am surprised, Miss Fitch, that you should have plighted your troth to one of these.'

'I was engaged to him once before. When I lived in Worcestershire.'

'Well, that's no reason why you should make a habit of it,' said Joe severely. He was much moved. 'You must get in touch with him immediately and break the engagement.'

'Oh, I couldn't.'

'Why not?'

'He would be certain to cry, and I couldn't bear it.'

'A dilemma,' said Mr Trout. 'Definitely a dilemma.'

'But I see a way round it,' said Joe. 'Has he a telephone?'

'Yes.'

'Then it's perfectly simple. You just ring him up and say "Is that you, Jaklyn? I'm phoning to say it's all off. I'm marrying Joe Pickering."'

Mr Trout frowned, clicked his tongue and tut-tutted.

'I could not endorse that procedure.'

'Why not?'

'The party of the second part would bring an action for breach of promise.'

'Men don't bring actions for breach of promise.'

'Men of Sir Jaklyn Warner's stamp do.'

'That's true. I wouldn't put it past him.'

'They have no shame. And we do not want Miss Fitch to run the risk of being mulcted in substantial damages.'

'Then what do you suggest?'

'That I go and see this man. The situation is beyond the scope of a layman. It needs a practised lawyer.'

'I call that a splendid idea,' said Sally, and Joe, though his personal tastes ran more in the direction of knocking Jaklyn down and jumping on him with hobnailed boots, had to admit that it was reasonable.

'I have handled many similar cases in Hollywood. My clients have often complimented me on my gifts of persuasion. But we must of course not lose sight of the fact that in the matter under advisement we shall be facing difficulties. I cannot guarantee success. I gather from the luxuriousness of this flat that you are wealthy, Miss Fitch. When I was in the living-room I noticed a Corot over the mantelpiece which must be worth a considerable sum. This Warner will not resign his claims willingly. One can only do one's best. But I will go and see him.'

'Now?'

'At once.'

'I'll come with you.'

'No. I must be alone.'

'Then I'll wait in the street,' said Joe.

'I see no objection to that,' said Mr Trout.

'Tell me,' said Joe as they started their journey. 'How do you propose to conduct these negotiations?'

'Just as I have invariably conducted negotiations of this nature,' said Mr Trout. 'From what you tell me of this Warner he appears to be no different from the impecunious young men of Hollywood with their diet of dry Martinis and sausages on little sticks. I have always found them amenable to a money offer and I have no doubt Sir Jaklyn Warner will be the same.'

'You mean to buy him off?'

'Precisely.'

'H'm.'

'You have doubts?'

'I was only thinking it's going to cost a bit.'

'Money well spent.'

'Yes, of course. No argument about that. The catch is that I haven't any money. But if you'll chalk it up on the slate, I'll repay you later. I shall have some coming in soon.'

The visibility in the cab was not good, but Mr Trout's benevolent smile did much to light it up.

'My dear boy,' he said. 'You surely do not suppose that I am going to charge you a fee or ask to be reimbursed for any expenses I may be put to on this case. I would not dream of it. As the colloquial expression has it, this is on the house. A small compensation for getting your affairs into, I must admit, a certain disorder. No true Californian would think of sending in a bill for services rendered to two young lovers in what practically amounts to Springtime.'

It was a moment before emotion would allow Joe to speak, so moved was he by the nobility of these sentiments. When he did speak, it was to pay a marked tribute to California, which, he said, judging from its inhabitants, must be quite a place. Unless, of course, Mr Trout was unique.

'Tell me,' he said. 'Are there any more at home like you?'

'There are a few,' said Mr Trout, 'and better boys you never knew.'

He winced a little as he spoke. He was thinking of Fred Basset and Johnny Runcible and G. J. Flannery, and wondering if his defection from Bachelors Anonymous would mean the break-up of a friendship of twenty years.

Chapter Thirteen

Things were not going too well with Jaklyn Warner. In addition to being married, to which he greatly objected, he had a nasty hangover and he owed a bookmaker fifty pounds. This was the debt he had had in mind when he told his future bride that he owed twenty. He had lacked the nerve to reveal the full amount to her.

The bookmaker, moreover, was not one of those kindly bookmakers with hearts of gold who can sympathize with a fiscally embarrassed young man and allow his account to remain unsettled indefinitely. Informed by Jaklyn that there might be a long delay before payment could be made, he had drawn in his breath sharply and looked grave.

'Oh, I do hope there won't be, Sir J.,' he said. 'I know it's silly to be superstitious, but I can't help remembering that every single client of mine that's done me down over money has had an accident happen to him. Time after time I've seen it occur. Time after time after time. It's like some kind of fate. Only the other day there was a fellow with a ginger moustache called Witherspoon. Owed me fifty for Plumpton and pleaded the Gaming Act. Less than a week later, would you believe this, he was found unconscious in the street – must have got into some unpleasantness of some kind – and had to have six stitches. No, seven. I was forgetting the one over his left eye.'

This conversation had taken place at the house of the creditor, and Jaklyn had left his presence feeling like a nervous young member of Captain Kidd's pirate crew who has just been handed the black spot. Arriving at his Chelsea residence, he found Mr Trout knocking on the door and beginning to get tired of achieving no result.

'Sir Jaklyn Warner?' said Mr Trout.

Normally if a caller had asked this question Jaklyn would

have replied in the negative, for he believed in taking no chances, but Mr Trout's aspect was so obviously that of one connected with the Law that he decided to risk it. He had prosperous relatives all over England, and one of them might quite easily have handed in his dinner pail, leaving him a bit of the right stuff, and this lawyer was here to tell him so.

'Yes,' he said. 'Who are you?'

'My name is Trout. Of the legal firm of Trout, Wapshott and Edelstein of Hollywood, California, in the United States of America.'

Jaklyn's hopes took a sharp rise. He remembered that his Uncle Eustace had left hurriedly for America at the time when he had been wanted by the police to assist them in their inquiries in the matter of a big long-firm swindle. He had always been fond of his nephew, and what more likely than that he should have fetched up in Hollywood, made a packet, perished of a surfeit of brandy smashes, and left that packet to that nephew. It was with a beating heart that Jaklyn put latch-key to door.

'Come in,' he said. 'Come right in.'

Following him over the threshold, Mr Trout was encouraged to observe the evidences of impecuniosity that met his eyes. A man with an abode as shabby as this, he felt, would surely be what he had called amenable to a money offer, and though he was prepared, if necessary, to spend cash lavishly on behalf of young lovers in what was practically Springtime, he hoped it would not be necessary. He had always been a man who liked to keep expenses down.

Taking a seat, he wasted no time on preambles.

'You are affianced,' he said, 'to my client, Miss Sarah Fitch.'

Another man in Jaklyn's position would no doubt have explained that owing to his having been the victim of what amounted to a shotgun wedding, marriage to Sally was no longer in the sphere of practical politics, but his native prudence restrained him. The sixth sense which had stood him in good stead from boyhood told him that this lawyer bloke's visit was somehow connected with money and that it would be rash to confide in him too freely.

'I am,' he said.

'Her father disapproves of the match.'

'He does, does he?'

'And he is prepared to pay you a reasonable sum if you will agree to consider it null and void.'

If Jaklyn felt that it was odd that Sally's father, a humble country vicar, should be in a position to scatter money about like this, he did not say so, feeling perhaps that the Reverend Fitch had won the Irish Sweep or backed a series of winners since he had last seen him. Nor did he protest, as some men would have done, that he had never been so insulted in his life. His thoughts riveted exclusively on the man with the ginger moustache and the seven stitches, he said:

'What do you call a reasonable sum?'

'Fifty pounds.'

'It's a deal.'

As Mr Trout had told Joe, this was not the first time he had had talks of this description with impecunious young men, but it was the first time an impecunious young man had reached a decision with such lightning speed, and it took his breath away. Fifty pounds had been what might be called his asking price, and he had taken it for granted that his mention of it would be the cue for the haggling to begin. Jaklyn's instantaneous acceptance of the offer gave him the feeling he had sometimes had when going downstairs in the dark and treading on empty space where he had supposed the last step to be.

His impulse on recovering his breath was to tell Jaklyn what a good man thought of him, but he had a dinner date with the woman he loved, and though she had warned him that she might be a little late in getting away from her hospital, he did not dare to spend time rebuking young men so lost to shame that censure would be wasted on them. He paid Jaklyn fifty pounds, and left in silence. And he had not gone far before emotional breathing made itself heard and Joe emerged from the shadows.

'Well?' said Joe. 'Did it go off all right?'

The anxiety in his voice amused Mr Trout. It seemed to him bizarre that his young friend should be entertaining any uncertainty as to the success of a mission entrusted to Ephraim Trout of Trout, Wapshott and Edelstein. He replied that it had gone off with the greatest smoothness. He had, as expected, swayed Jaklyn Warner like a reed, bending him to his will with eloquence which there was no withstanding. Warner could see from the firmness of his manner that argument would be futile and that no nonsense would be stood.

Joe gave him a worshipping look.

'Trout, you're a marvel!'

'One does one's best, Pickering.'

'It's a knack, I suppose, this ability of yours to look people in the eye and make them wilt?'

'I would prefer to call it a gift.'

'You're probably right. Anyway, thanks again. I wish there was something I could do for you.'

'There is. You can give me a word of advice.'

'What's your problem?'

'I am dining tonight with Mrs Bingham, and I would like you to brief me as to the advisability of proposing marriage to her.'

Joe in his uplifted mood was feeling that the world would be a better place if everybody started proposing to everyone. He said it struck him as splendid idea.

'You do not think it would be too soon?'

'How do you mean?'

'An exhibition of masculine impetuosity might frighten her.'

'I doubt it.'

'I have not known her long.'

'Incompetent, immaterial and irrelevant. Women like a dashing man.'

'Is that so?'

'Why, it's only a year or two since man used to snatch women up on their saddle bows and ride off with them. And the women loved it. A pity you can't do that.'

'A great pity.'

'But nowadays, of course, they expect you to propose. The great thing is not to do it over the soup. Wait for the coffee. Where are you dining?'

'At the Dorchester.'

'I'll drop you there.'

'Very good of you. Why not over the soup?'

'Not romantic.'

'Of course, of course, of course. I might have made a grave blunder. Thank you, Pickering.'

'Not at all. Go to it, Trout, and heaven speed your wooing.'

It was in the spirit of the Polish gentleman in the song who sang 'Ding dong, ding dong, ding dong I hurry along, for it is my wedding morning' that Joe, having deposited Mr Trout at his destination, took the cab on to Fountain Court. If you wanted to be finnicky about it, it was not actually his wedding morning, but this made no difference to his euphoria. Admitted by Sally to number 3A, he folded her in a close embrace, waltzed her four times round the room and informed her that this was the maddest merriest day of all the glad new year because the dark menace of Sir Jaklyn Warner, Bart, had ceased to operate.

'Everything is fixed up,' he said. 'No wedding bells for you.'

'I know,' said Sally. 'He's married already.'

Once more Joe found himself gripped by that peculiar feeling of having been struck on the bridge of the nose by a wet fish. He relaxed the folded embrace and stared incredulously.

'He's *what*? Who told you that?'

'Daphne. She's the one he married. She told me just after you and Mr Trout had left.'

'Who's Daphne?'

'Daphne Dolby. She lives with me.'

'Oh, the personable popsy,' said Joe, recalling Jerry Nichols's remarks.

'She is personable,' said Sally, 'but that's not why Jaklyn married her. I think I had better explain.'

'If you don't want me to have a dizzy spell.'

'It's quite simple really.'

'To a brain like yours, perhaps, not to mine.'

'Daphne was engaged to Jaklyn.'

'One of those easy to please girls?'

'She was all set on becoming Lady Warner.'

'Oh, I see.'

'So when I told her I was engaged to him, it naturally made her think a bit. She decided she had to move quickly, or she would lose him, because I was a much better bet from Jaklyn's point of view than she was. I had just been left twenty-five thousand pounds.'

'Yes. Jerry Nichols told me about that.'

'Great added attraction, twenty-five thousand pounds. So she took him to the registry office and made him marry her.'

'Yes, I get the picture now. She sounds like quite a girl.'

'She is.'

'We must have her to dinner some night when we are in our little home.'

'And it will be a very little home, I'm afraid.'

'Meaning what?'

'That's all we shall be able to afford. Oh, Joe,' said Sally, 'I've made the most awful fool of myself. I'm the world's worst half-wit.'

Chapter Fourteen

Joe frowned.

'You are speaking of the woman I love,' he said stiffly.

Sally continued in the depths.

'But will you after you hear what I've done?'

'Will I what?'

'Love me.'

'Certainly I will. Love conquers all, as Trout would say. Oh, by the way! Trout.'

'What about him?'

'We've got to be very careful what we say to Trout. He must never know about Jaklyn being married. He thinks his triumph over him was due entirely to his eloquence and the force of his personality. It would give his self-esteem a nasty sock on the jaw if he learned the awful truth.'

'I don't see why we should be fussy about Trout's feelings. He nearly ruined our lives.'

'But with the best intentions.'

'As it is, he's probably ruined mine.'

'How do you figure that out?'

'All through him I may have lost you.'

'What gives you the idea that you may have lost your Pickering?'

Sally gulped. The moment had come for confession, and confession was as unpleasant to her as it is to most people.

'How much does money matter to you, Joe?'

'Very little. Dross, I sometimes call it.'

'Would you still want me if I hadn't any?'

'Don't ask foolish questions.'

'You would?'

'Of course I would.'

'Well, that's a relief. Because I haven't.'

There are observations, popularly known as conversation-stoppers, which are calculated to cast a hushed silence on the most animated dialogue. One might have supposed that this would have been one of them, but Joe, though startled, received the news with equanimity. The truth was that in spite of Jerry Nichols's assurances he had not been able to overcome a certain uneasiness at the thought of the wide gap between Sally's finances and his own. Pure though his motives were in seeking to make her his bride, he had had the uncomfortable feeling that people who did not know those motives might place him in the Jaklyn Warner class. Thanks to Mr Llewellyn, that modern Santa Claus, this uneasiness had ceased to trouble him. He was able to speak with perfect calmness.

'You haven't any money?'

'No.'

'But what's become of it all? You can't have spent twenty-five thousand pounds on chocolates and ice cream since last Tuesday.'

Sally smiled politely, but it was a painful smile. Confession was still to come, and she hated it more than ever.

'Did Mr Nichols tell you about my legacy?'

'Not in any detail. I happened to mention to him that I loved you, and he said "Oh, the heiress", adding that somebody had left you a packet.'

'Yes, Miss Carberry. I told you about her.'

'The anti-tobacco woman you once worked for.'

'Yes. She left me the money on condition that I didn't smoke. And Daphne Dolby was to live with me to see that I didn't. If she caught me smoking, it was all to go to the Anti-Tobacco League. So I was careful not to smoke.'

'Very prudent. Very sensible. But I feel there is more to come.'

'There is. Tonight I did. I had a cigarette.'

'With the Dolby prowling and prowling around like the troops of Midian!'

'She wasn't prowling around. That's the whole point. She went out about five minutes after you and Mr Trout left. She forgot to take her cigarette case with her. It was lying on that little table there. It caught my eye, and suddenly I felt I would die if I didn't have a smoke. It was all Trout's fault.'

'That's the part where I don't quite follow you. I don't see how Trout comes into it.'

'It was the way he talked. Don't you remember? All that stuff about being unable to guarantee success because we must not lose sight of the fact that in the matter under advisement we should be facing difficulties. He made it sound as if he hadn't a hope.'

'Lawyers always talk that way. You should hear Shoesmith of Shoesmith, Shoesmith, Shoesmith, and Shoesmith. It's their native caution. Building for the future, as you might put it. If the thing's a flop, they can say "I warned you that this might happen." If it's a success, you will think how wonderful they must be to have brought it off against all the odds.'

'Well, I didn't know that, so he left me a quivering mass of nerves –'

'But looking terrific.'

'– and I was just wondering how I could pull myself together and shake off this awful feeling of depression, when my eye fell on Daphne's cigarette case.'

'And you reached for it?'

'I reached for it.'

Joe nodded understandingly.

'Just what any girl would have done in your place. And the Dolby remembered her case and came back to get it and found you blowing smoke rings?'

'Yes.'

'I thought as much. I am a playwright, and we playwrights have a sort of sixth sense. Well, when I say I'm a playwright, *Cousin Angela* did have sixteen performances. Many a dramatist has to be content with opening on Friday and closing on the following Saturday. And talking of *Cousin Angela* . . .'

'She was as hard as nails about it.'

'Talking of *Cousin Angela* . . .'

'You might think that as we had become friends she would have pretended not to notice, but when it has anything to do with her job she has no friends.'

'Very praiseworthy. But I was about to speak of *Cousin Angela*. I have a bit of news which may bring the roses back to your cheeks. Llewellyn is going to do it as a picture.'

He was right about the roses. They returned just as predicted. Sally emitted what in any popsy less personable would have been a squeal.

'You might have told me before,' she said reproachfully.

'Slipped my mind.'

'I've been going through hell.'

'Good for the adrenal glands.'

'How much?'

'We haven't talked terms yet.'

'But these studios always pay the earth, don't they?'

'Invariably.'

'We shall be rich without my money.'

'Modestly bloated.'

'And no danger of your feelings being hurt because I paid the bills.'

'The husband always ought to have the money. Ask any husband.'

'Yes. Otherwise it offends his *amour propre*.'

'My God. French and everything. I'm getting a gifted wife. You must have been on many a day excursion to Boulogne.'

'I did go once.'

'You didn't happen to run into a man named Bingham, did you?'

'Not that I remember.'

'You would have remembered if you had. He fell overboard. You would have noticed. Well, excuse me for a moment.'

'Where are you going?'

'Only to the telephone. I thought I ought to ring Llewellyn up and ask him how he's getting on. He's in hospital.'

'Is he ill?'

'No. Merely hiding from Vera Dalrymple. I'll explain later.'

From her knowledge of Ivor Llewellyn, gathered at the time when she had interviewed him for her paper, Sally would have supposed that any telephone conversation in which he took part would have been of considerable duration. She had thought of him as a man always with plenty to say and not averse to the sound of his own voice. But this telephone conversation terminated almost before it had begun. Joe said 'I.L.? Pickering,' and that was all he said. And after listening for not more than a minute he hung up and came away from the instrument, Mr Llewellyn having apparently replaced the receiver at the other end.

It perplexed Sally. Then she saw Joe's face, and perplexity was succeeded by dismay.

'Joe!' she cried. 'What is it?' and he smiled the ghost of a twisted smile, the smile of a man whose world has collapsed beneath him but who knows that he must show himself one of the bull-dog breed whose upper lips never unstiffen.

'Do you want it broken gently?'

'No!'

'It'll be a shock.'

'I don't care.'

'Well, I'm sorry to say Llewellyn has fired me and isn't going to do the play.'

Sally did not swoon, but looking back later she wondered how she had managed to avoid doing so. The floor heaved like an ocean swell, and Joe became for a moment two Joes, both flickering. It seemed an age before she could speak, and when she did she could only say 'But why?'

Joe replied that Mr Llewellyn had not told him why.

'All he said was "Pickering, eh? Just the man I wanted to contact. You're fired, Pickering, and if you think I'm going to make a picture of your damned play, you're mistaken." '

'Nothing else?'

'Only instructions to remove my blasted belongings from 8 Enniston Gardens without delay.'

'But what had you done to him?'

'Not a thing.'

'Had he seemed hostile?'

'On the contrary, my stock was particularly high with him. He wanted to avoid Vera Dalrymple, who had phoned to say she was coming to call, and I suggested that he should go to hospital. His gratitude was touching.'

'Well, I don't understand it.'

'I do. It's the jinx that's been following me around for weeks, making everything I do go wrong.'

'Not everything. You found me.'

'But we can't get married.'

'Why can't we get married? Try to stop me.'

'What'll we live on?'

'I've got a job.'

'I haven't.'

'You'll get one.'

'Who says so?'

'I say so. We'll be all right. All it needs is prudence and economy. And now go and get your things, and then you can take me out to dinner at Barribault's. You owe me a dinner at Barribault's.'

Joe, as he reached journey's end, was feeling somewhat, if only a little, better. Agony though it was to be parted from Sally even for a moment, there was something, he felt, to be said for being alone and free from interruptions. He had much on his mind, and the solitude of 8 Enniston Gardens allowed him to think.

One of his subjects for thought was of course the mystery of the sudden animosity of Ivor Llewellyn, which, as Sherlock Holmes would have said, undoubtedly presented certain features of interest. For when a man has thanked you – and in broken accents, at that – for showing him the way out of an unpleasant dilemma, you do not expect him five minutes later, or practically five minutes later, to start treating you like a leper who has tried to borrow from him.

But in these bustling times one is seldom permitted to remain uninterrupted for long. Scarcely had Joe set the little grey cells to work on the Case of the Inexplicably Annoyed Motion Picture Magnate than the telephone rang. With a sigh and wishing that he had someone, as Mr Llewellyn always had, to whom he could say 'Answer that. If it's for me, say I'm out', he reached for the receiver, and a familiar voice spoke.

'Joe?'

'Oh, hullo, Jerry.'

'I'm phoning to ask if everything went off all right. I must say I didn't expect to find you at Enniston Gardens. I thought you would have been at Fountain Court.'

'I'm going back there.'

'Did things go according to plan?'

'Yes.'

'You followed my advice?'

'Yes.'

'Close embrace?'

'Yes.'

'Till ribs squeaked?'

'Yes.'

'Result, complete reconciliation?'

'Yes.'

'You don't sound very ecstatic.'

'I've got a spot of Llewellyn trouble.'

'Is that all?'

'It's enough for me.'

'Don't let it get you down. These things always iron themselves out. It's like when my father starts throwing his weight about. We just sit tight and let him rave, knowing that he will eventually come off the boil and resume his place in the comity of nations. And now I must leave you, Joe. In fact, I must rush. I'm putting on the nosebag with a popsy.'

Jerry withdrew, but the truth of the old saying that if you particularly want to be left undisturbed to brood over your problems the telephone is sure to ring was exemplified once more a moment later. This time it was Mr Trout.

'Pickering? A hearty good evening to you, Pickering. Glad to find you in, Pickering. You might have been out, and I want a word with you.'

Even though separated from him by a length of wire Joe had no difficulty in diagnosing the speaker's mental state. Mr Trout's voice was the voice of one who, putting his fate to the touch to win or lose it all, has found himself a winner. Its volume made that plain. No man, Joe felt, to whom the adored object had handed the pink slip could so nearly have fractured his ear drum, and forgetting his own troubles for the moment he rejoiced in the other's good fortune. Mr Trout might be the sort of man whose morning post was never without its quota of attractive offers from lunatic asylums, but he wished him well.

'I gather from your manner,' he said, 'that you have offered your heart with good results. Over the coffee?'

'No, Pickering, over the oysters. I couldn't wait for the coffee. Swallowing my fifth oyster, I snatched her up on my saddle bow, ha ha, and carried her off. We are going to have coffee after I have finished telephoning. I was hoping to get Llewellyn.'

'He's in hospital.'

'So Amelia told me. She was his nurse. But he is not in hospital. I phoned St Swithin's, but he had gone.'

'Gone?'

'Leaving no trace. Some trouble about somebody wanting a sample of his blood. One supposes that he is on his way to Enniston Gardens. Well, if he comes, I want you to tell him about me and Amelia. Tell him tactfully, for it will be a shock.'

'Why?'

'Because, as she was leaving the hospital, he asked her to marry him.'

'You don't say!'

'On the contrary I do say. And she told him she would think it over. Think it over! Ha,' said Mr Trout. 'I didn't give her much chance to think it over. I must have electrified her.'

Joe gave him an admiring look, its effect, of course, largely diminished by the fact that they were talking on the telephone.

'I told you women liked a dashing man.'

'How right you were.'

'You and Errol Flynn, not much to choose between you.'

'I suppose not.'

'Give my respects to the future Mrs Trout.'

'I will.'

It now needed only Mr Llewellyn to make the little circle of Joe's intimates complete, and shortly after Joe had said good-bye to Mr Trout the roster was filled. There was the sound of a turning key, and Mr Llewellyn walked in, looking a little ruffled, as if he had just escaped from a hospital against the wishes of its staff. His hair was disordered, and he had omitted to put on a tie.

Even to an unobservant eye it would have been apparent that he was not one of Joe's admirers. In the look he gave him as he entered there was something of the open dislike which a resident of India exhibits when he comes to take his morning bath and finds a cobra in the bath tub. Not even at the nurse who wanted to take a sample of his blood had he directed a more formidable glare.

'Oh, it's you,' he said.

Joe conceded this.

'What are you doing here? I told you to get out.'

Joe said he had been collecting his belongings.

'As instructed,' he added. He spoke curtly, for since their talk on the telephone he had not been well pleased with his former employer, deprecating his habit of firing good men simply, apparently, to gratify a passing whim.

'And do you know why I told you to get out?'

'I've been trying to think.'

'I'll tell you.'

Mr Llewellyn had swelled like a bull-frog, and his glare had intensified in animosity. A sense of grievance often has this effect.

'Because you officiously insisted on my going to that damned hospital, when you must have known what would be the result if I did. This afternoon the inevitable happened. I asked my nurse to marry me. She said she would think it over. One can scarcely suppose that having thought it over she will not say Yes. No woman I've ever asked to marry me has not said Yes. There is something irresistible about me. Tomorrow, therefore, I shall be engaged, and from there to being married is but a step. I'm not saying anything against Amelia Bingham, she's a very good sort, but I don't want to be married, and thanks to you I shall be. And you wonder why I've fired you. Why are you grinning like a halfwitted ape?'

He was referring to the gentle smile which had appeared on Joe's face as he heard the name Amelia Bingham.

'May I say a word?' said Joe.

'No.'

'It's just that –'

'I don't want to hear it.'

'It's simply –'

The telephone rang.

'Answer that,' said Mr Llewellyn. 'If it's for me, say I'm out.'

Joe, though half inclined to say 'Answer it your ruddy self', did as directed, and was surprised to hear the voice of that great lover Mr Trout. He had thought Mr Trout would be otherwise occupied.

'Pickering?'

'Yes.'

'Is Llewellyn there?'

'Just come in.'

'Have you told him?'

'Not yet.'

'Let me speak to him. It will come as a shock to the poor fellow to hear that I have won Amelia from him, but he only has himself to blame. The idea of letting her think it over. You don't win a woman that way. The way to win a woman –'

'I know. Saddle bow stuff.'

'Exactly.'

Joe handed the receiver to Mr Llewellyn.

'Trout,' he said.

Watching Mr Llewellyn as he telephoned, Joe was not surprised to see his face light up shortly after he had addressed Mr Trout as Benedict Arnold and asked him if he had sold any good forts lately. His share of the conversation after that was mostly gasps and gurgles, but it was soon evident that good relations had once more been established between him and his old friend. When he replaced the receiver, his face wore the expression which one notices on the faces of those who have been saved from the scaffold at the eleventh hour, and his voice when he spoke had so much of the carolling skylark in it that Percy Bysshe Shelley, had he been present, would have been fully justified in saying 'Hail to thee, blithe spirit'.

'Don't tell me miracles are no longer box office,' he chanted.

'How wrong I was in supposing that my guardian angel was asleep at the switch. Do you know what?'

'Yes.'

'Amelia Bingham is going to marry Trout.'

'Yes. That's what I was trying to tell you.'

'It's colossal!'

'Yes.'

'It's sensational.'

'Yes.'

'Don't be so damned calm about it, Pickering. You don't seem to realize what this means to me. Would you care to have a rough scenario of my future plans? I shall return immediately to California, where I shall become a member of Bachelors Anonymous. Trout is giving me a letter to a friend of his named Runcible, and he assures me the boys will welcome me with open arms. Gosh, I feel like a million dollars!'

Joe laughed one of those hollow, mirthless ones.

'I dare say you do,' he said, 'but I don't.'

'What's the matter with you?'

'You aren't going to do my play as a picture.'

'Who says so?'

'You said so.'

'Hell's bells,' said Mr Llewellyn, astounded. 'You surely don't believe everything the top man of a motion picture studio tells you? I remember now, I was feeling a little sore with you at the time, and I expressed myself with the generous strength which is so characteristic of me, but you don't have to pay any attention to that. Of course I'm going to do your play. We've only to settle terms. How about two hundred and fifty thousand dollars?'

Joe rose from six to eight inches into the air with a hoarse cry, and Mr Llewellyn misread his emotion. He had so often heard stars cry hoarsely like that in response to an offer. Coming from Joe, who was not a star, it piqued him.

'Dammit,' he said, 'you can't expect top prices for your first picture. Two hundred and fifty thousand isn't at all bad, ask anyone. Take it or leave it.'

'I'll take it,' said Joe.

'Good. Come and have some dinner.'

'I was giving my fiancée dinner.'

'I'll come along,' said Mr Llewellyn, who knew the pleasure his company was bound to add to a meal.

It was as at Joe's suggestion he completed the writing and signing of a rough form of contract that the doorbell rang, and his torso and both his chins shook in sudden alarm.

'Vera Dalrymple!' he gasped.

Joe did not share his tremors. There had been a time when he had trembled with fear at the lady in question's frown, but with that contract in his pocket and the air vibrant with wedding bells he felt more than equal to a dozen Vera Dalrymples.

'Leave her to me, I.L.,' he said. 'Go and hide in the bathroom or under your bed or somewhere. I'll attend to her.'

And with a firm step he strode to the door.

More About Penguins
and Pelicans

Penguinews, which appears every month, contains
details of all the new books issued by Penguins as they
are published. It is supplemented by our stocklist,
which includes around 5,000 titles.

A specimen copy of *Penguinews* will be sent to you free
on request. Please write to Dept EP, Penguin Books
Ltd, Harmondsworth, Middlesex, for your copy.

In the U.S.A.: For a complete list of books available
from Penguins in the United States write to Dept CS,
Penguin Books, 625 Madison Avenue, New York,
New York 10022.

In Canada: For a complete list of books available from
Penguins in Canada write to Penguin Books Canada Ltd,
2801 John Street, Markham, Ontario L3R 1B4.

Evelyn Waugh

This *enfant terrible* of English letters in the 1930s
became a best-seller with the publication in 1938 of
his first novel, *Decline and Fall*. Many of the
characters in this masterpiece of derision reappear
in the subsequent novels, which, culminating in
Put Out More Flags, present a satirical and
entertaining picture of English leisured society
between the wars.

Evelyn Waugh books in Penguins are:

Black Mischief

Brideshead Revisited

Decline and Fall

The Loved One

Men at Arms

Officers and Gentlemen

Put Out More Flags

Scoop

Vile Bodies

Unconditional Surrender

A Handful of Dust

The Ordeal of Gilbert Pinfold

When the Going was Good

Work Suspended and Other Stories

P. G. Wodehouse in Penguins

'Mr Wodehouse's idyllic world can never stale. He will
continue to release future generations from captivity
that may be more irksome than our own. He has made
a world for us to live in and delight in' – Evelyn Waugh
in a B.B.C. broadcast

*The following are some of the titles by P. G. Wodehouse
published in Penguins:*